KYRA AND THE SALOON BOSS

BLUEBONNET BELLES
BOOK ONE

BROOKE STANTON

COCO& BEE

To my cats
Ted Lasso, Chief of Lap Operations
Shelby Shannon, Director of Keyboard Interruptions

1

KYRA

889, Wylde, Texas

"Honey, you lost?" A handsome, middle-aged woman with hair as black as soot and loose curls about her shoulders descended from the stage, the worn saloon floorboards creaking with each confident step. She had the kind of presence that commanded attention and was dressed in a worn-out ruffled hoop skirt, a style which had gone out with the war twenty years ago.

Kyra checked the crumpled letter in her gloved hand and swallowed over the dust that had clung to her since she boarded the stagecoach in Oklahoma City.

"Is this the Bluebonnet Hotel?" Her voice was almost drowned out by the relentless twang of a fiddle and the rhythmic stomp of boots. The warmth of the Texas spring, so unlike the chilly Maine she'd left behind, trickled sweat down her back, making her wool dress feel more like a punishment than proper attire.

Kyra had entered the humble hotel through the lobby, but when no one was there to greet her, she'd followed the music into the attached saloon.

"You found it, honey. Though I'm guessing this ain't quite

what you expected." The woman's eyes, sharp as a hawk's, flicked over Kyra, taking in her disheveled state.

"I'm looking for Sarah Bailey." Kyra glanced at the four young women on the stage, but none of them could be her aunt. They were far too young, dolled up with bright rouge and scandalously short skirts.

"Goodness, that's a name from the past." The woman's fingers dug into Kyra's elbow and roughly pulled her to the far side of the stage. "I'm Scarlett. Now, who might you be?"

"Kyra Anne Bailey. Sarah's my aunt. On my mother's side." She hoped the explanation would be enough to stop the woman's scrutiny, and it may have worked because Scarlett's gray eyes widened with delight.

"Well, I'll be damned," Scarlett said, a slow smile curving her lips. "You're Sarah's kin. I see it in that stubborn hold of your chin. Follow me, sugar."

They walked to the long, weathered bar, scarce of patrons at this midday hour. Scarlett pulled out two stools, placed two cloudy glasses in front of them, and expertly filled them with a clear liquid.

"Drink up." Scarlett held up the small glass and took the shot.

Kyra lifted it, sniffed, and dropped it back to the bar, her nose burning. "Do you have any lemonade?"

The woman laughed, fine lines crinkling the sides of her eyes. She reached into an icebox and poured the yellow liquid on top of the alcohol. "That'll take the edge off."

Kyra took it and drank, puckering her lips at the bitter taste.

"Do you know my aunt?" Kyra asked, squirming in her seat, her backside sore after four days of sitting on trains, carriages, and coaches.

Scarlett's eyes twinkled with something like amusement. "Oh, I know her alright." She leaned back, hiking up her skirts as she settled on her stool. "Now, what's a pretty thing like you doing in a place like this? Your aunt's the madam here. Do you know what that means?"

"I'm aware of my aunt's vocation. It's why I came." Kyra wiped her cheeks roughly. She knew she looked a mess—blonde hair gritty and mussed, dirt on her dress and face, gloves stained—but adrenaline shot through her body. She hoped the long and arduous journey had not been for nothing. "I'm here for a job. My husband's run out on me, and I'm left with nothing. If working here is good enough for Aunt Sarah, it's good enough for me."

Scarlett's smile faded slightly as she poured herself another drink. "You sure about that, darling? This ain't no place for a lady."

Kyra shifted under Scarlett's quiet assessment. She didn't blame the woman. It probably wasn't often, if ever, a lady walked into a brothel and demanded work. But Kyra hardly felt like a lady. She'd played the part of a professor's wife these past five years, but she never fit in with the well-mannered, polite society that came with her position. She often found herself in the lecture halls of the university, soaking in the knowledge and pretending she was one of the students at the co-ed college.

Not that this dusty town fit her any better. Kyra didn't know where she fit in in the world, but she certainly knew it was no longer—and never had been—a wife to Henry Hadley.

"I understand your meaning, and that's why I've come," Kyra said. "I can't remarry. My husband may have disappeared, but technically I'm still bound by our marriage. I won't work in a factory making my hands bleed for pay that won't even cover rent in a hovel—if working here is my means to independence, I'll do what I must to survive."

Kyra took the bottle, slugged a gulp from it, and slammed it down, making her point. "I'm not some delicate flower. I understand what it means to be a Bluebonnet Belle."

"You've got spirit, I'll give you that," Scarlett said, letting out a hearty laugh that echoed off the saloon walls. "Not the innocent little girl I remember. You're naive as a newborn calf, but there's fire in you."

Kyra blinked, the realization hitting her like a runaway coach. "Aunt Sarah?"

"That's right, girl. But everyone calls me Scarlett here. No one's called me Sarah since—"

Kyra flung herself into Scarlett's arms, the embrace so forceful it sent them both tumbling off their stools and onto the floor in a tangle of skirts and laughter.

"Oh, I'm so sorry." Kyra untangled her limbs from her aunt's, but their skirts and ankles were caught up around each other.

"Roll left, dear." Scarlett tugged the crinoline of her skirt, and Kyra rolled roughly across the sticky floor, only to bump into a pair of polished boots, the impact sending a jolt of pain through her ribs.

"You alright down there, darlin'?" a deep voice drawled above her, rich with a Southern lilt.

Kyra rolled to her back and flung her gaze upward. Towering over her stood a man as out of place in this saloon as she felt. Tall, with a tailored suit and a bowler hat perched at a rakish angle, he exuded an air of authority that was impossible to ignore. His spectacles glinted in the low light as he bent down to offer her a hand.

"I ... I'm fine," she stammered, scrambling to her feet and dusting herself off, all while avoiding his outstretched hand. She could feel his eyes on her, judging, as she awkwardly scooted back toward Scarlett.

The man bent forward and scooped up Kyra's grimy bonnet. "I believe you lost this."

"Thank you," Kyra mumbled, yanking it from his hand and shoving it back onto her head.

The man glanced around the saloon as if he were sizing it up, taking note of every nook and cranny.

Scarlett, the picture of composure, slid back onto her stool with a graceful ease that belied their undignified tumble. "May I help you, sir?" she asked, her voice all honey and charm. "A drink, perhaps? Or something a bit more ... satisfying?"

The man's lips pulled into a frown. "I'm not here for pleasure, ma'am. That's my brother's vice, not mine."

Kyra's mouth hung open, but Scarlett smiled wider. "My girls are clean as a whistle that's never been blown."

The man raked his gaze over Kyra's rough appearance.

"She's not one of my girls," Scarlett said, pouring a drink for the stranger. "She's my niece."

"All the same, I'm here on business." He took off his hat, revealing light brown hair, slightly damp with sweat, and wiped his forehead with the back of his hand. "I need to speak with the manager."

"You're looking at her." Scarlett smiled, nudging the drink toward him. "Miss Scarlett Bailey. You may call me Scarlett. No formality here."

The man blinked, clearly taken aback. "You run this place?"

"Disapprove of a woman running things?"

"No," the man said, taking Kyra by surprise. "I'm only shocked my brother didn't."

Scarlett's smile vanished. "Who's your brother?"

"Clive Kent," he said, adjusting his glasses, reminding Kyra of the professors she used to watch and admire. But there was nothing she found to admire about this man.

"That scoundrel's your brother?" Scarlett asked, her voice steel beneath the sweetness.

"Yes, ma'am. I'm Declan Kent."

"Well, I'll be. Your brother's been missing for weeks. I had to step in and keep things running." Scarlett crossed her arms over her chest, matching his grit. "Why are you here, Mr. Kent?"

Mr. Kent's expression hardened. "To inform you that my

brother is no longer owner of the Bluebonnet. I am." He knocked the shot back without losing eye contact with Scarlett. "And I'm shutting this place down."

2

DECLAN

"You can't!" the younger of the two women screeched, slamming the tips of her booties against the steel toes of Declan's boots and craning her dirt-smudged face to look up at him, her hands on her hips. The smell of sweat and dirt and days of travel wafted off her, and he took out a kerchief and placed it under his nose to block the stench.

"What's your name, girl?" Declan asked calmly. He'd dealt with worse than her.

"Mrs.—er, Miss Kyra Bailey," she said with a quick glance to her aunt. There was something suspicious about her, but he didn't care enough to press the issue. He had business to attend to that had nothing to do with this pathetic creature. Her hair was greasy and matted to her temples, and this close he could see a smattering of freckles peeking through the grime on her cheeks.

"Miss Bailey, kindly step aside so I may resolve this matter promptly with Miss Scarlett."

She didn't budge.

"Do you have papers saying as much?" Miss Scarlett asked calmly, stepping between Declan and the grimy woman.

Declan opened his leather satchel and produced the documents that he'd procured the day before. His brother, Clive, had been in a brawl in Frisco, the next town over, and he'd shot the deputy. The young man survived, but Clive landed himself in jail, awaiting a trial.

He'd written Declan and begged for money for his bail, but instead of sending him the funds, Declan had traveled from Lexington, Kentucky to deal with his brother directly. Declan was done letting his brother drill his life into the ground. There was always some hole to dig Clive out of.

As the oldest son of a fatherless family, Declan was the patriarch—a role he stepped into at twelve. In order to provide for his family, he took his first job as a secretary for an accounting firm. Declan had always been good with numbers. He liked the simplicity of them. They never lied. He'd worked his way up and now worked as an accountant for a large bank.

"Looks legit." Miss Scarlett handed the papers back to Declan, but Miss Bailey snatched them, reading them over.

"I agree," Miss Bailey grumbled, and Declan snorted in disbelief.

"You know something about the law, miss?" Declan asked with a smirk.

"A fair amount, sir," she said with a confidence that made Declan falter.

"Regardless of what that paper says, you're not shutting us down," Scarlett said.

"You have no say in this matter." Declan stepped past the women. There was chittering near the small stage. Several young women huddled together, watching the scene. They wore short dresses and a ghastly amount of rouge.

"Are these the whores?" Declan asked.

"The Bluebonnet Belles," Miss Scarlett said smoothly. "They're dancers and servers and, when the price is right, ladies of the night."

"They're no longer needed," Declan said to Miss Scarlett, then turned to the young women by the stage and spoke louder for them to hear. "You may pack your things. This establishment will no longer need your services."

There was a collective gasp, and one of the women began to whimper.

"Ladies," Miss Scarlett spoke to them. "You're not going anywhere."

Heat raced up Declan's neck and prickled his scalp. What the hell did this woman think she was doing? "I said they are dismissed. I do not need their ser—"

"Mei, step forward," Miss Scarlett said, cutting Declan off in a sharp tone.

A young woman with coal-black hair, straight as a horse's mane, stepped forward. Her features were soft, her skin like buttermilk, her eyes pinched at the corners. "Why are you a *whore*?" Miss Scarlett spoke sweetly, but there was iron in her tone.

"My dad disowned me and kicked me out."

"Why?" Miss Scarlett prompted.

Declan crossed his arms and waited. If they wanted to put on a show to try and persuade him, let them. His mind would not be changed. He had to sell this place if there was any chance of saving his brother. His original intent in coming down to Wylde was to teach his brother a lesson. But Clive's situation was more dire than he'd realized.

"My father forced me to marry the only other Chinese man in town. He's forty years my senior. A drunk. Gambled all his money away. Makes me do this to pay his debts." Her face hardened as she spoke of her husband.

"And when Mr. Kent fires you, what will you do then?"

"My husband will be furious. To keep the money coming in, he'll sell me to his friends and debt collectors. Without the protection of Miss Scarlett and this establishment, I'll be dead in a year." Mei shuddered, fear shadowing her features.

"How do we protect you?" Miss Scarlett asked what Declan was thinking.

Miss Bailey, the grubby young woman, leaned in, her gaze fixed on Mei, taken in by the story.

"There are rules about harming the women who work here," Mei said. "Good fortune is on our side inside these walls. Miss Scarlett made sure of that."

"Thank you, Mei," Miss Scarlett said, signaling for another girl to step forward.

"Enough," Declan sighed. "I don't need—"

"Jewell," Miss Scarlett said, stepping on Declan's words. Another young woman strode to the forefront of the stage. She was shorter, with ash-brown skin and curly hair piled atop her head . "What will you do when Mr. Kent forces us to close down?"

"I reckon I'll return to New Orleans where I lived before and after the war." She spoke softly, but her gaze was hardened.

"The war was twenty-five years ago. You can barely be that age now," Declan said, wondering if these women were spinning tales.

"I was a babe then, yes. But when we were freed, my family stayed on as house servants. Once I was old enough, I came here. Mr. Camden, my old master, would eagerly take me back. He was furious when I left."

"Is he a kind man?" Scarlett asked gently.

"He beats the servants and starves them when he is not pleased. The master's son is kind. Taught me to read. But his papa is a mean son of a gun. Momma says it ain't Christian, but she hopes the Lord takes Mr. Camden before his rage kills someone."

"She can't go back there," Miss Bailey cried out, her hands gripping her belly protectively. "Mr. Kent, don't hurt these women."

Declan's jaw tightened. How dare she. He'd never lay a hand on a woman, but their misfortunes were not his fault.

"I suppose I could sleep outside, beg for food, and pray someone has mercy on me," Jewell continued, looking directly at him. "But I'm no beggar. I'll go back to work in that house if you make me, though I'll be treated no better than the barn cats."

"No," Miss Bailey said, her cheeks reddening under the dirt. "How can you stand there with a scowl on your face while these women speak of the horrors they'll face? The Bluebonnet Belles are famous. Nearly as famous as Madam Brezing's Palace in Kentucky. It shouldn't be a punishment to be born a woman." Miss Bailey's voice caught, and tears pricked her eyes. "Why do all men have to be so cruel?"

She bit her lip and turned away from Declan, her slight shoulders shaking. A sharp pain accosted his chest. His whole life he'd tried to protect the women in his family from the men in their lives. His mother had been abandoned by his father, taking every penny and valuable when he left. And Declan's sister was trapped in an awful marriage.

It's why he needed to sell the saloon. Declan's bank had been hit by the economic depression that ruined many people's lives in the past decade, and the money he'd need to save his brother would wipe out his savings.

Declan fisted his hands and cursed under his breath. Miss Kyra Bailey unnerved him, but her tears squeezed at his better nature. Her silvery eyes told of a darker story, and her words held desperation.

She was right. He could not be the reason for the cruelties that would certainly come upon these young women if he shut them down. That was certain. When he'd forced his brother to give him the deed, he hadn't realized what he'd stepped into.

"I *will* sell the saloon, but—" Before he could continue, Miss Bailey spun on her heels and, to his shock, she hammered her small fists into his chest.

"Is your heart stone?" she yelled.

Declan snatched her wrists and held her before him. She wrestled against his grip but soon gave up, the exhaustion of her effort overtaking her.

"Woman, shut your mouth and listen," Declan barked, jostling her aside.

"I will sell this place, but"—he put his hand up, shutting her protests down—"I will not close the brothel while I look for a seller. After that, it'll be up to the new owner what to do with you."

Miss Scarlett, who'd kept a keen eye on Declan during these past few minutes, smiled wryly. "And?" she asked. "What's the catch?"

She was right. There was more.

"Until then, it'll be my rules," Declan said, raising his eyebrows, challenging her or Miss Bailey to disagree. "I want to know how every inch of this place is run. From the finances of the bar to the business of the brothel. I can see you take great pride in what you've built, Miss Scarlett, but it's mine now. And I shall choose what is fit to stay and what must go in order to get the best price."

Miss Bailey's smile was tight, but her hand, which gripped her belly, relaxed.

"Fair enough," Miss Scarlett said and put out her hand. Declan dismissed it.

"This isn't a deal between us. This is my hotel. But I'm not a fool. You've gained the trust of those who work here, and I imagine you know the intimate details of all the folks in this town. I'll need that knowledge. And as for you, miss," Declan said, turning his attention to Miss Bailey, "I may not know much about the prostitution business, but you're not fit to be a whore. Not in this state. And if you strike me again, you'll be out on the streets. I don't care what your wretched story might be. Then I shall be the cruel man you've accused me of."

"Don't you worry about her," Miss Scarlett said, shuffling a glowering Miss Bailey behind her. "I'll find something useful for her to do."

"I already have a job for her." Declan kicked the large case next to him. "Miss Bailey, take my things to my room."

"Pardon?" she asked, looking at the bags as if they were poison.

"For the time being, you will be my clerk, maid, valet, whatever I desire. I shall pay you, but I expect you to be at my beck and call or you'll be back on a coach to Maine."

Her icy gaze could've frozen the creek that ran through the town, but she curtsied and said, "Yes, sir. Whatever you wish, sir."

Declan's gaze narrowed, not trusting the sweetness in her tone or her swift compliance. "I'll be keeping a keen eye on you, Miss Bailey."

Her gaze was unfaltering. "And I you, sir."

3

KYRA

Kyra stormed through the lobby, her heart rattling like a stampede, every step echoing the maddening rhythm of her frustration. Ahead of her, the detestable Mr. Declan Kent swaggered as if he owned the place—which, technically, he did.

Her fingers tightened around the strap of her satchel in one hand while in the other she clutched Mr. Kent's ridiculously oversized case. She resisted the urge to hurl it at the back of his head. Instead, she glared daggers into his broad shoulders, still reeling from his announcement, the words echoing in her mind —he was selling the Bluebonnet.

"I'll show you to your brother's rooms," Scarlett said, her tone sweet as pie, leading the way. Kyra's stomach turned. How could her aunt, of all people, cater to this horrid man?

This was meant to be the start of Kyra's new life, and this brute had barged in and threatened to ruin it all.

As they climbed the wide staircase, Kyra's knuckles whitened as she squeezed the case even tighter. Mr. Kent followed Scarlett, and Kyra trailed behind, seething with each step. Tall, smug, and utterly insufferable, Mr. Kent was a walking reminder of everything she despised. He glanced back and caught her eye for a moment. Making sure she hadn't run, Kyra scoffed in her mind.

His stern gaze held hers, and her breath caught. Oh, curse it. He was handsome in that rough, unpredictable sort of way that made a woman wonder just how dangerous he was.

Enough of that, Kyra. He's the enemy.

She hadn't rid herself of the chains of one man only to be latched to another.

"Mr. Kent," she called out, forcing her voice to remain steady despite the turmoil bubbling within her.

He turned at the top of the steps, and their gazes locked. For a brief, infuriating moment, she lost herself in the striking blue of his eyes, the kind of blue that was far too unsettling to belong to a man like him. She pulled herself together before she did something ridiculous, like sigh.

"I'll assist you today," she said, the words clipped, "but tomorrow I have other duties. Isn't that right, Aunt Scarlett?"

Scarlett paused a few steps ahead where the hallway split. Kyra silently begged her aunt to back her up, to save her from this unwanted task. But before Scarlett could answer, Mr. Kent leaned forward, his eyes gleaming with amusement. "Other duties? Do tell, Miss Bailey. I'm dying to know what exactly you do here because it's obvious you're not a whore. Do you drive cattle? Is that why you're such a mess and carry your satchel?"

Kyra's jaw clenched. "That's none of your business."

"Everything here is my business now," he replied smoothly, his voice as arrogant as his smirk.

Scarlett placed a soothing hand on Kyra's arm, as if she could tame the fire raging inside her. "Kyra, darling, you can assist Mr. Kent. Just for now. Until we figure out what's what."

Kyra shot a look at her aunt, disbelief simmering in her chest. "So, you're siding with him?"

Scarlett sighed, the kind of long-suffering sigh that made Kyra feel like a petulant child. "No one's taking sides, sugar. But we've got to be practical."

Scarlett gestured down the left hallway. "This side is where the girls conduct their business," she explained, her tone even, as if this were all perfectly normal. "And over here"—she pointed in the opposite direction—"are the rooms for our hotel guests. Including your brother's apartment, Mr. Kent."

Mr. Kent gave the girls' hallway a long glance before turning to follow Scarlett. As he did, his smaller satchel slipped from his hand.

"Grab that, will you?" he called over his shoulder, not even bothering to slow his pace.

Kyra's eyes narrowed into slits. He did that on purpose. With a grunt, she snatched up the bag under her arm, fighting the urge to toss it over the banister.

They stopped in front of double doors, which Scarlett unlocked. Inside the first room was a large study, the desk cluttered with papers, books, and inkwells. Past it lay another room with a double bed, a wardrobe, and a dresser.

Kyra heaved Mr. Kent's luggage onto the mattress and dropped her satchel to the floor.

"Unpack my bags and meet me at the bar. We'll discuss your tasks there." Without waiting for a response, he strode out, Scarlett in tow.

Kyra stared after him, her body taut with rage. She approached the bed, her steps heavy with anger, and flung open his case. Half-full, thank the heavens. That meant he didn't plan on staying long. But then, as her fingers brushed against the smooth leather of his shaving kit, an idea—a wicked, delightful idea—sparked.

Before she could talk herself out of it, she snapped the blade of his razor in two, sliding the pieces into her pocket. A petty act? Perhaps. But the satisfaction it brought was worth it.

Once she was done, she descended the stairs and found Mr.

Kent exactly where she expected—leaning casually against the bar, sipping whiskey, laughing with the barkeep.

She marched up to him, her pulse hammering in her ears. "I've unpacked your bags," she announced, her voice rising with the fire inside her. "Now, if you don't mind, I shall freshen up. I know my appearance offends your delicate sensibilities."

Mr. Kent blinked, then smiled a slow, lazy smile that made her want to slap him and kiss him in equal measure. "There's no need to be dramatic, Kyra."

"Miss Bailey," she snapped, her patience at its end.

"Miss Bailey it is, if it pleases you," he said with a mocking twinkle in his eye.

"What would truly please me, Mr. Kent, is you packing your bags and leaving." She crossed her arms, daring him to argue. "My aunt doesn't need you here. You can sell this place through a solicitor. There's no need for you to stick around."

Mr. Kent leaned back and regarded her with an arrogant tilt of his head. "That's not how it works, *Miss Bailey*."

"It could work that way," she challenged, knowing the law better than most men, thanks to her days spent in the lecture halls and law library.

"That's not your concern." His smile dropped, and he regarded her with a stern gaze. "Now go fetch your aunt. I need to speak to her."

Kyra bit back a retort and stalked away. She held her head high, but inside a storm brewed. She had not been in town one day, and already she worried she'd made a grave mistake. Mr. Kent was dead set on making her his puppet, and she'd had enough foul men for a lifetime.

She sucked down a deep breath, gathering her wits as one thing became crystal clear—Declan Kent might think he could waltz into her life and control her fate, but he had no idea what he was up against.

4

DECLAN

The evening sun stretched long fingers of light across the wooden floorboards of the Bluebonnet Saloon as Declan strode in, his boots striking a heavy rhythm. The afternoon had been a blur of telegraphs to regional and national newspapers, informing them of the sale—tedious, but necessary.

He'd also penned a letter to Clive's lawyer up in Frisco, requesting an update on the trial and, more importantly, any mounting fees. Declan needed the sale of this damn place finalized before the end of the trial. He had no time to argue with his brother over money. Not this time. *If* Clive returned.

Clive had always been the kind of trouble that latched on like burrs to a dog's coat. Declan was always the one left pulling them out. As the eldest, he'd been cleaning up Clive's messes since their father disappeared. Someone had to protect their mother from the heartache her youngest constantly brought home.

Their sister, Isabella, had been the easy one. Until she married that monster. Another mess Declan was determined to clean up. But this time, Declan feared it might be too late. If Clive couldn't find a way out of the noose, it would break their mother. Declan would move mountains to spare her that pain, even if it meant locking his brother up for a stretch to knock some sense into him. *If Clive's fate didn't lie in the gallows.*

The saloon's raucous energy pulled him from his thoughts, the lively tune from the piano mingling with the clatter of poker chips and shouted bets. Declan scanned the crowd, immediately noting one very important absence: Miss Kyra Bailey.

All morning, she'd been stuck by his side, a reluctant but surprisingly efficient companion in sifting through the tangled mess of bills and finances. Between the hotel, the saloon, and the brothel, it had been a hell of a job—far more convoluted than he'd expected. He had to give it to her, though; the woman was sharp, even if she grumbled the whole way through. But her dark mutterings amused him.

He'd told Scarlett to give Miss Bailey the room across from his, for convenience. Though when Miss Bailey had brought him breakfast that morning, still in the dusty clothes from the day before, he'd finally reached his limit. The smell alone had been offense enough to order her to bathe before he returned. Surely that wasn't too much to ask of a lady, was it?

Yet now, as he scanned the saloon, she was nowhere in sight.

His gaze settled on Mei, the young Chinese girl draped over a cowboy at one of the poker tables. Her bosom practically spilled out of her dress, and the cowboy forgot about his hand entirely, his eyes locked on her as though she were the ace he desperately needed.

"Excuse me, Miss Mei," Declan spoke, stepping next to her. She straightened up instantly, her hand drifting to his collar as if it were second nature, adjusting it with a small smile on her crimson lips.

"Yes, Mr. Kent," she purred.

Mei was a pretty little thing—petite, with ink-black lashes and lips the color of fresh cherries—but Declan had no interest in what she was offering. He took a step back, making the distance clear. "Have you seen Miss Bailey?"

Her smile turned sly as she leaned forward, her lips brushing the air near his ear. "I believe she's resting in her room."

Declan nodded, ignoring the heat in his collar as he took his leave. He headed for the stairs, his boots hammering the wooden planks as he climbed them, two at a time.

He'd been perplexed that she hadn't already had a room, but Scarlett had explained that Miss Bailey was a new arrival, like him. Her husband had run out on her. Declan couldn't blame him. She was an impossible woman.

At Miss Bailey's room, the door was ajar, and a flicker of light from inside revealed two figures. Scarlett, with her ever-confident presence, stood talking to a young woman sitting on the edge of the bed. Declan paused just outside, curious about this unknown lady.

Her hair, a golden cascade, was styled in an elegant updo, and her stylish dress shimmered in the dim light. He could only see part of her face, her delicate fingers worrying at the fabric of her skirt.

"I've been with a man. I was married, after all," the young woman said, her voice laced with uncertainty. "But ... is there more to it than just the act?"

"How did you and your husband lie together?" Scarlett asked, her tone patient yet knowing.

Was this a new painted lady in training?

The young woman bit her lip, her cheeks reddening. "I would lie there while he, uh, did his business on top of me." She shrugged helplessly. "Isn't that what most women do?"

Scarlett let out a low, sardonic laugh. "That's what most wives do. But that's not what whores do. There's far more to it than just what's between your legs."

"Oh my."

Declan froze. That voice. He squinted, straining to get a better look. When the young woman shifted, his heart clenched as he realized the poised, golden-haired beauty in front of him was Miss Kyra Bailey herself, scrubbed clean and nearly unrecognizable.

How was this the same woman who had snarled at him all morning like a wet cat? And now, she was asking Scarlett about ... forbidden subjects? Good God, this was not a conversation he should be overhearing or that a decent young lady should be participating in.

He told himself to walk away, but his boots stayed rooted to the spot, his breath hitching as Scarlett spoke again.

"You'll learn soon enough. There's much more to pleasing a man than simply spreading your knees."

"Oh." Miss Bailey's eyes widened, but there was also determination. "Very well, then. I may as well learn it all. Can I start tonight?"

Declan's blood pounded in his ears, an inexplicable fury bubbling within him, and he slammed the door open, startling them both.

"Absolutely not!" he thundered, the sound reverberating through the room.

Miss Bailey shot to her feet, her face a mixture of shock and fury. "How dare you listen to our conversation!" she hissed. "You, sir, are no gentleman!"

He strode into the room, his anger barely contained. "I own the Bluebonnet Belles," he growled. "And I say no."

Miss Bailey's eyes sparked with defiance. "My personal choices are none of your concern, Mr. Kent."

His jaw tightened at her audacity. "When it interferes with your duties to me, it most certainly is."

Scarlett, ever the coolheaded one, stepped between them. "Mr. Kent, perhaps you should join us tonight. It would help you better understand the business you're so eager to sell."

Declan blinked, caught off guard by the suggestion. His fury began to ebb, but what replaced it was something far more confusing—a mixture of curiosity and disgust, and something else he didn't dare name.

Scarlett was right. If he intended to sell this place, he needed to know every detail of how it ran, so he pushed his misgivings aside.

"Very well," he said, his voice gruff as he nodded.

Miss Bailey huffed, sweeping her skirts with an exaggerated flick, sending a waft of her flowery perfume toward him as she started toward the door. "Wait," Declan said, "we're not actually ... watching the transactions, are we?"

Scarlett pressed her lips together, a glimmer of amusement in her eyes. "Not tonight, sir. But if you're curious, arrangements can be made. You're welcome to any of the girls."

Heat rose up his neck as Miss Bailey chimed in, "Any girl but me."

"You are the last woman I'd bed, Miss Bailey." He scowled.

To his surprise, Scarlett turned sharply on Miss Bailey. "The first lesson you must learn, dear child, is to bite your tongue around the clients. No matter how displeasing they may be."

Miss Bailey frowned but gave a stiff nod.

"But," Scarlett continued, sashaying down the hallway, Miss Bailey and Declan following, "in my establishment, except for the rare occasion, the women may reject an offer. But don't expect that to happen often—most are eager for the money."

Scarlett stopped at the top of the steps.

"Tonight we'll keep it tame," she said. "But you are correct, Mr. Kent. If you want to understand how this business works in its totality, you will have to watch a few transactions. Eventually."

Miss Bailey threw him a self-satisfied glance. "If you're not too chicken, that is."

Declan ground his teeth, fighting the urge to respond. She was infuriating. Infuriating and yet, damn it, if she didn't look so damned good in her clean frock and tidied appearance.

"I hope this confidence translates to the bedroom, my dear niece. You're going to need it," Scarlett said, her words swiping the smug look from Miss Bailey's face. "The clients expect more than just a woman who can lie on her back."

"And I look forward to my lessons," Miss Bailey said with an impish smile. Unbidden, an image of Miss Bailey undressed on a bed entered Declan's mind, and blood rushed into his groin.

He had not agreed to Miss Bailey being a whore, but she was the least of his concerns, and so he said nothing. As long as it didn't interrupt her duties to him, he'd allow it. For now.

Without a farewell, Declan hurried down the stairs, running from the uncomfortable feelings low in his belly, and from these sordid women.

5

KYRA

Kyra would be lying if she said she wasn't terrified of this new life she'd chosen. But was it even a choice when women like her had so few options beyond begging or bending to the will of men?

She'd spent the night shadowing Mr. Kent and Scarlett, who'd taught him the ropes of running the Bluebonnet Belles. Scarlett was a master of charm, juggling the men and the girls like a ringmaster, while Kyra tried to keep her jaw from dropping at the sheer audacity of it all.

The saloon was rowdy, as expected, but the rougher edges had surprised her. A few card games had turned ugly, but Scarlett always had a way of defusing tension with a smile and a strategic hand on a man's arm.

What truly caught Kyra off guard was the sight of Jewell stepping out of a room with a nasty bruise darkening her cheek.

Mr. Kent had stepped forward, his fists raised. His fury had surprised Kyra. She thought he'd look the other way.

"We'll ban him," Scarlett had said, her tone sharp, stopping Mr. Kent's involvement. "We do our best to keep the fights at the bar."

Jewell had just shrugged, unconcerned. "I've had worse."

Still, Scarlett made sure the man paid double before he left the premises.

The next morning, as Kyra sat cross-legged on her bed, shoveling a biscuit into her mouth, she couldn't help but ask, "How do you stop men from hurting the girls? Men can do whatever they want with little consequence."

Mr. Kent was in his room bathing—thankfully—which gave Kyra the chance to ask Scarlett these questions before his inevitable barking of orders resumed.

Scarlett, seated on the edge of the bed, sipped her coffee with a calm that Kyra envied. "I slip the sheriff and a few other key men in town a cut of the profits. They keep an eye out for trouble. Not all men are bad, Kyra. Not all hit."

Kyra snorted into her biscuit. "You must be acquainted with a different breed."

Scarlett raised a brow but let the comment slide. "Everyone in town knows if you mess with one of my girls, there'll be hell to pay. We've had a few incidents, sure, and we're always cautious with the travelers. But this is one of the safest brothels in Texas. I make sure of it."

Scarlett smiled, setting her cup down with a soft clink. "Tonight, you'll sit in on one of the transactions."

Kyra choked, coughing biscuit crumbs across her bed. "Already?"

"We may not be around much longer," Scarlett replied, adjusting the sleeve of her simple, mint-green dress. It was a far cry from the extravagant gown she'd worn the night before, her makeup-free face making her look years younger. "Better to learn fast."

Kyra's stomach flipped at the thought. "What happens if the new owner shuts this place down?"

Scarlett shrugged, the picture of nonchalance. "I'll pack up the girls and move west to one of the new rail towns. Start over, same as I always do. But it'll take time to build trust and secure their safety. Nothing's guaranteed, Kyra. Not in this business."

As Scarlett cleared their breakfast plates, nudging the door open with her elbow, she added, "We'll have a mini lesson tonight before things get busy. And trust me—there's no lying on your back like a starfish with your tits out in my brothel."

A deep voice cut through the hallway behind her. "Bite your tongue, woman. There's no need for such crass language."

Mr. Kent, his damp hair disheveled after his bath and his spectacles pushed up on his nose, stood glowering at them from the doorway.

Scarlett shot him a wicked grin as she sauntered past. "Oh, honey, that was nothing. Join us tonight for one of the transactions and find out what this bawdy house is really about." She patted his shoulder, leaving him standing there, visibly flustered.

Kyra couldn't help herself. "You're blushing, Mr. Kent."

His blue eyes blazed with irritation. "Shut your mouth, Miss Bailey. Scarlett may get away with her casual talk, but I'm your boss. Displease me, and you'll be out on your backside. I need Scarlett. I don't need you."

Kyra's face burned, and her fingers clenched at the sheets. The nerve of the man! But he wasn't wrong. He could toss her out, and she'd be left with nothing. The thought chilled her.

"Come with me," he said brusquely, shoving a small notepad and pencil into her hands. "We're inspecting the entire establishment. Write down everything I say."

Over the course of the day, Kyra followed Mr. Kent as they toured every corner of the hotel, from the guest rooms to the management office, the kitchen to the pantry, and then the saloon. They inventoried the liquor, checked the state of the furniture, and finally ventured into the quarters where the girls slept and worked.

Most of the girls were still in bed when Mr. Kent barged in, but they obliged him with sleepy smiles, showing Kyra and him around their rooms. Each was uniquely decorated—some elegant, others more modest—but all carefully maintained. Mei explained that each girl washed her linens daily, spritzed perfume on the beds, and sponged herself down before every shift.

"No bedbugs or disease in my establishment," Scarlett said proudly from the doorway of Mei's room. "Most working men don't care about the state of things so long as they can get what they came for. But I care. And so do certain wealthier gentlemen who frequent the Bluebonnet. I run a clean, respectable business, and I aim to be a destination, just like Madam Brezing's place in Kentucky."

Kyra looked up, curious. "Why do you call your girls the Blue-bonnet Belles?"

"Because they're as pretty as the bluebonnets in Texas," Scarlett said with a wink. "Plus, I like the alliteration."

Mr. Kent raised an eyebrow, clearly impressed. Scarlett merely smirked. "Yes, Mr. Kent, I'm an educated woman. Shocking, I know."

Once they'd finished the tour, Scarlett clapped her hands together. "Grab some supper from the kitchen, then meet me back in my room. It's time for the next part of Kyra's education. I want it done and out of the way before the clients come. And, Mr. Kent," she added with a playful whisper, "I'd recommend leaving your morals outside that door. You won't be needing them tonight."

Mr. Kent stiffened, his broad shoulders growing even more rigid. Kyra suppressed a grin, gleeful at the discomfort on his face.

Maybe tonight wouldn't be so bad, if only to see Mr. Kent squirm.

~

"First, do we all know the parts of a woman's and a man's bodies?"

The evening's "class" began with Scarlett standing before the small group, a large sketchpad in hand. Kyra sat in a chair next to Mr. Kent, while Mei, Jewell, and a redheaded girl named Maeve perched on Scarlett's large bed.

Scarlett flipped open the sketchpad to reveal two rather detailed anatomical drawings—one of a man and one of a woman.

Mr. Kent shot to his feet so fast, his chair crashed into the dresser behind him. His mouth opened to protest, but the bemused looks from the women silenced him. Cheeks flushed, he sat back down.

"This feels highly inappropriate," he muttered.

Scarlett paid him no mind. "We'll focus on the male anatomy first since our job is to satisfy his desires."

Kyra clamped her hand over her mouth, her eyes widening as Scarlett explained every inch of the male body in exacting detail —from the foreskin to the head, to the delicate ball sacks, and even the less-discussed areas. Kyra's face colored, while Mr. Kent's hand shielded his eyes as if he could block out the images.

"Are we all still breathing?" Scarlett asked, barely suppressing a grin.

"Horrified," Mr. Kent mumbled.

"Fascinated," Kyra said, and she meant it. Her mind had always veered toward learning and this was teaching her biology and human relations in a way she'd never imagined.

"I'll quickly go over the woman's anatomy. Maeve, do you mind?"

Maeve leaped off the bed, and with a few swipes of her fingers, she'd unbuttoned her flimsy dress and it fell to the floor, exposing her naked flesh. Maeve was Irish. If her accent didn't give it away, then her ivory skin, dotted with freckles, surely did. Her alabaster skin practically glowed in the lamplight.

Mr. Kent tensed beside Kyra, but, to his credit, he kept his eyes steady on Maeve. Scarlett began to map out the parts of a woman's body, moving between the sketch and Maeve's bare form.

"This is the most sensitive part of a woman, much like the head of a man's penis," Scarlett explained, pointing to something called the clitoris, and Kyra leaned forward, captivated. "If stimulated the right way, a woman can achieve her own release. Some men enjoy watching a woman reach her peak. Would you like a demonstration?"

Without waiting for a response, Scarlett placed her fingers on Maeve's clitoris, and she let out a breathless moan.

"Enough!" Mr. Kent jumped to his feet, knocking his chair over again. "This is—I can't—pardon me." He rushed from the room, his fists clenched, and Kyra caught a glimpse of the bulge straining against his trousers.

"Was that his ...?" Kyra began, trailing off in disbelief.

"It seems Mr. Kent may need to pay one of my girls a visit tonight," Scarlett chuckled. "If he doesn't take care of it himself."

Kyra blinked, unsure what Scarlett meant by that, as the other girls fell forward in a fit of giggles.

"Don't worry, honey." Scarlett winked. "I'll explain everything."

6

DECLAN

eclan hustled into his room, slamming the door behind him as if he could shut out the chaos churning inside his body. His manhood throbbed, pressing against the front of his trousers uncomfortably, and he cursed under his breath, taking slow, deep breaths. He tried to will his body into submission, but the desire coursing through him was relentless, his fingers twitching to give in to the aching need.

Was he so easily undone? One look at a naked woman and he was about to disgrace himself like some green lad. His cock pulsed, defying him, and he clenched his jaw.

He was thirty-three years old and still untouched. He'd never had the luxury of indulging in women. The only nudity he'd ever witnessed had been through faded sketches of the female form and ancient paintings in dusty books. Practical. Predictable. Unlike the fiery heat that had ignited in him as he'd listened to the so-called lessons, watched that young woman being touched.

He wasn't prepared for this. For any of it.

As the sounds of the brothel and saloon hummed outside his door—men bellowing, women laughing, the shuffle of feet on wooden floors—the pulse between his legs began to ebb, cooling his heated thoughts. The blood retreated, leaving him frustrated and confused.

Damn it. What had he gotten himself into?

Declan was a man of numbers. An accountant at a respectable bank. Ledgers. Calculations. He could tally a profit margin faster than a man could draw his pistol, but this ... this world of flesh and temptation was foreign territory. And yet, Scarlett insisted that to truly grasp the business, he had to witness what these women did.

But to watch the act itself? He didn't know if he could. It made his skin crawl with both anticipation and dread.

He couldn't admit to anyone here how green he was—never having touched a woman. Men in Louisville frequented whore-houses and found mistresses to take care of their needs, like anywhere else, but Declan had never imbibed.

A knock at the door pulled him from his thoughts.

"Mr. Kent?" Scarlett's voice was soft but steady. "Are you in there? The women are on stage right now, and once the first show is done, the other evening activities will commence. Would you like to join me in watching how a deal is struck and, most importantly, how I keep my girls safe?"

Declan hesitated, but it was essential he grasp all aspects of the business. He opened the door to find Scarlett smiling with that unnerving mixture of kindness and knowing. If she suspected why he'd fled earlier, she made no mention of it, and for that, he was grateful.

"How exactly do you keep them safe?" he asked, his voice rougher than usual as he stepped into the hallway.

Scarlett led him down the stairs as she spoke. "As I told you, I have important men like the sheriff and his deputies on our side. They get first pick of the girls and a cut of the earnings in exchange for protection. But that's not all." She glanced at him. "I hire guards to stand at the end of the hallway. Each room has a pull cord that rings a bell. If trouble starts, those men come running with their guns drawn. They are intimidating even without their pistols."

"And if the girls can't reach the cord?" Declan asked, frowning.

"The guards walk the halls regularly. They check through the peepholes in the doors. So far, we've only had one serious problem, but we handled it."

Declan raised an eyebrow. "Only one?"

"Since I put these safeguards in place, yes." Scarlett's tone was matter-of-fact. "I make sure the men know the rules before they step foot in a room. No rule following, no visit."

Declan's mind whirled with questions, but one stood out. "And these guards? They've never caused trouble themselves?"

"They're well paid," she said simply. "Men do a lot for the right price."

Before they entered the bustling saloon, Declan stopped her. "You mentioned that the women have the right to refuse a man. Doesn't that create complications?"

Scarlett gave a wry smile. "Rarely. My girls aren't fools. They're whores by trade, and refusing a paying customer isn't something they do lightly. But, on occasion, they exercise that right."

Declan shook his head, still trying to wrap his mind around how this place operated. It wasn't like the brothels he'd heard whispered about back home in Kentucky.

As they entered the saloon, the music from the stage blared, and the women—their costumes scanty—danced provocatively, kicking their legs high and flashing glimpses of the dark hair between their thighs. The men closest to the stage leaned forward eagerly, eyes gleaming with lust.

Declan meandered through them until he reached the bar. The bartender, a young Irish man called Bryan, whom Declan had met the night before, placed a glass in front of him. "Whiskey?"

"Rum," Declan said. He'd need his senses dulled if he was

going to get through this night. And he was determined to get through it with his cock bridled.

Declan shot the warm liquid back and asked for another, sipping it on a stool next to Scarlett. A few feet from where he sat was Miss Bailey. Her wide eyes were glued to the stage, watching the women. Scarlett, on the other hand, surveyed the men in the room with the calculating gaze of a hunter, sizing them up.

At the end of the bar, a man in a sharp suit sat nursing his drink, his eyes fixed on Mei. A businessman, Declan guessed, likely one of the railroad men. Scarlett, who wore a bright red dress with ruby lips to match, swayed her hips over to the gentleman. Declan and Miss Bailey followed Scarlett but settled on stools several feet away so they could overhear but not interfere.

"You like the way she rocks her hips? They don't just move to music," Scarlett purred, nodding toward Mei as she motioned for Bryan to refill the man's drink. "She's quite talented. My best girl. And since you're the first customer of the evening, I can offer you a special deal and you'll get her before anyone else."

The businessman's gaze slid from Mei to Scarlett, his eyes raking over her from the hem of her dress to the top of her hat.

"Would you like to put your feet up in her room? You won't have to lift a finger unless you want to, and she'll take very good care of you." Scarlett leaned in, her voice dropping to a low, intimate murmur. "Every inch of you."

The man nodded once, a silent agreement, and Scarlett signaled for Jewell and a large, burly man named Lorenzo. Jewell quickly led the gentleman upstairs, while Lorenzo followed close behind to ensure everything went smoothly.

Scarlett repeated this ritual with several other patrons before turning her attention to Bryan. "I have a special task for you tonight, Bryan. Can you ask George to take over?"

An older man who had been stocking the bar and clearing the tables slid behind the bar, giving Bryan a brief nod.

"What do you need, ma'am?" Bryan asked, his brow furrowing in confusion.

"I need you to help with a private demonstration in the bedroom," Scarlett replied with a sly smile. "Jewell will be your partner. Miss Bailey and Mr. Kent will watch."

Bryan's face paled, his mouth opening and closing like a fish out of water. "M-me, ma'am?"

"You," Scarlett confirmed. "Jewell will take care of you. Just follow her lead."

Bryan cast a quick, excited glance at Jewell. "O-okay, ma'am."

"Go with Jewell. She'll get you fixed up in her room, and we'll be right there."

As Bryan scurried off, Declan shot Scarlett a questioning look.

"Is he going to be alright?" Miss Bailey asked, wringing her hands together.

"Oh, don't worry, honey," Scarlett replied with a laugh. "Bryan's been begging for a chance to be with Jewell since he started here, but he hasn't had enough coin for her company. Tonight's his lucky night."

Declan's discomfort grew, his fists tightening at his sides as they followed Scarlett up the stairs.

"Most customers don't want an audience," Scarlett explained over her shoulder. "Hence, the need for Bryan tonight. I want you both to see how things work in a more controlled environment."

As they reached the top of the stairs, Miss Bailey tripped, and Declan instinctively reached out, his hand gripping her elbow to steady her. She glanced up at him, her usual fire dimmed by a flicker of apprehension.

"I thought we were watching a real transaction," Declan said, his voice low as he released Miss Bailey's arm.

"Oh, it'll be real enough," Scarlett replied with a mischievous glint in her eye as she opened the door.

7

KYRA

Kyra followed Scarlett into Jewell's room, her heart pounding fiercely in her chest. The space was small but feminine, with a bold touch—purple velvet curtains draped the lone window, and white lace decorated the surfaces. Despite its size, the bed dominated the room, wide and inviting, though what it invited was something Kyra wasn't sure she was ready for.

Jewell stood beside the bed, her skimpy dress leaving little to the imagination, her full breasts spilling over the top of a tightly laced corset. Kyra's gaze flicked to Bryan, who lay on the mattress, his trousers embarrassingly tented, and she gasped, realizing what that bulge was.

"Typically, we have to do a little work before we get that result," Scarlett said with a sardonic smile, "but it seems Bryan here is eager to get started."

His cheeks bloomed crimson, but his eyes gleamed with a mixture of nervous anticipation and excitement.

"Most of the time, the man will already have his hands on you before you've even closed the door," Jewell said, her voice steady despite the roughness of her words. "Some men won't even bother to undress you. They'll just hike your skirts and push in."

Scarlett let out a dry laugh. "True enough. But some like to take their time."

"I don't think our subject here will be one of those," Jewell replied, a teasing lilt in her voice as she brushed a black curl from her face.

Bryan gave an apologetic smile. "I'm sorry, miss."

Jewell placed a gentle hand on his shoulder, her voice soothing. "Oh, darlin', it wasn't an insult."

Kyra clamped a hand over her mouth, holding back a laugh.

"Now," Scarlett began, her tone turning instructional, "a man might want to undress you himself, and depending on your outfit, you may have to help him."

She turned Jewell around, displaying her corset and skirt for Kyra's benefit. Before Scarlett could continue, Mr. Kent pulled a chair over from the vanity and sat down, legs crossed, pulling out his ever-present notepad.

"Carry on," he said, adjusting his spectacles as if he were ready for a lecture.

Scarlett raised an eyebrow. "This lesson is more for Miss Bailey, but if you must take notes, go right ahead."

"I want to understand it all," Mr. Kent said, pushing his glasses up his nose with a determined air.

Normally, spectacles would detract from the handsomeness of a man, but on Mr. Kent they looked studious, even scholarly, in a way that titillated Kyra.

It annoyed her immensely.

Scarlett instructed Bryan to untie Jewell's corset, his fingers fumbling with the ribbons as he struggled to undo the intricate bow.

"Never laugh at the client or make them feel small," Scarlett advised. "If he can't manage, do it yourself. If you can't, pull the bell and ask one of the guards to get me, and I'll assist."

Bryan managed to undo the bow and immediately got to work loosening the laces. When it was done, he yanked it off. His hands went straight for Jewell's breasts, kneading them like a loaf of bread, and Jewell winced. It did not look pleasant.

Kyra's stomach churned. Could she endure such rough handling? She'd have to. This was her path now, her only shot at freedom.

Scarlett placed a gentle hand on Bryan's shoulder. "If you think the man will not take offense, you can ask him to be gentler."

Bryan immediately complied, his fingers brushing softly over Jewell's breasts. Her dark nipples hardened in response, and a little moan escaped her lips.

"But," Scarlett added, her voice sharp, "if you sense bruising his ego would cause trouble, let him be."

"Trust me. When their pride is injured, it doesn't go well." Jewell nodded, leaning into Bryan's hands.

Kyra glanced at Mr. Kent, who sat behind her, his brow furrowed as he watched the scene unfold. His focus was unnerving, as though he were studying a ledger rather than a bawdy demonstration.

"As Scarlett said, the man usually wants to get straight to business. They aren't concerned with your pleasure," Jewell explained, shimmying out of her skirt. "Although some men surprise you."

"Like me, miss. I want to make you feel good too," Bryan quickly said, his hands still fondling her breasts.

Jewell bit back a grin. "Um, thank you, Bryan."

"Lie down," Scarlett instructed, and Bryan did so with surprising quickness. Jewell yanked his pants down, revealing his manhood standing at full attention between his thighs.

Kyra gasped, her hands flying to her face. She had never seen a man so ... exposed.

"You're not going to learn much from behind your hands," Scarlett quipped.

"Sorry." Kyra forced her hands down, her pulse racing as she took in the sight again.

"It's okay, Miss Bailey," Bryan said with a goofy grin. "I don't mind."

Scarlett eyed him for a moment before asking, "Bryan, have you ever been with a woman before?"

Bryan's face colored deeper. "Well, uh ... Miss Penny and I ... once."

"Oh." Jewell and Scarlett exchanged a look. "She hasn't worked here for over a year."

"That was my only time," he admitted, squirming slightly on the bed. "And it was, um, quick."

Kyra's gaze was glued to Bryan's member, fascinated to see it unencumbered. This encounter was very different compared to the perfunctory coupling she'd endured with her husband. Henry had never let her see much of anything. He'd simply yanked her close, lifted her skirt, and done what he needed to do. But this ... this was something entirely different.

Kyra leaned forward, and Bryan's member twitched in response.

"Oh!" Kyra jumped back, bumping into Mr. Kent's knees. Their eyes met for a split second, and she quickly looked away.

"It moved," she whispered, astonished, doing her best to ignore Mr. Kent's closeness. It was unnerving to have him here during this intimate encounter.

"It does that sometimes," Scarlett chuckled.

Kyra swallowed hard, a strange heat coursing through her body, pooling in her belly.

"Jewell, will you demonstrate how you use your mouth to give pleasure?" Scarlett turned to Kyra. "This is a top request, so pay attention."

Jewell leaned over Bryan's hips. Her right hand scooped up his member, pulled back the foreskin, and placed him into her mouth.

"Oh God!" Bryan yelped.

Kyra's heart slammed in her chest, and her hand fisted in front of her mouth. She'd never imagined such a thing. Her husband had certainly never asked for it.

"This is typical?" Kyra asked, her voice barely above a whisper.

"I doubt many gentlemen are asking it of their wives," Scarlett said, her tone dry. "But for whores? It's common enough."

Bryan panted as Jewell continued, his face flushed with pleasure. "Oh my ... oh ..."

Jewell released him with a wet pop, and Bryan's eyes shot open in surprise, his gaze darting between his glistening manhood and Jewell's lips.

"Wait," he pleaded, breathless. "Aren't you going to—"

"Don't worry. You'll have your release," Jewell said, swiping a loose strand of hair from his forehead.

"First, I want Kyra to see what it looks like for a woman to reach her climax. Not because you need it for this line of work, but if it happens, I don't want you to be shocked. You should always be in control of your body and of the client." Scarlett turned to Kyra with a knowing look. "Have you ever had a climax, Kyra?"

She shook her head. Kyra didn't know what Scarlett meant.

"And you, Mr. Kent. Have you seen a woman in the throes of ecstasy?"

Mr. Kent's grip tightened around his notebook. "That is not your concern," he replied stiffly.

Kyra wondered if Mr. Kent was being modest or if he was like her husband and only cared about his own pleasure. She turned back as Jewell's hand slid between her legs to her womanhood, and her fingers slowly rubbed the top of her mound. Bryan sat up, watching Jewell in open wonder.

"May I?" Bryan asked, reaching for her.

Jewell took his hand and placed it on her. At his touch, she sucked in a short breath, and she guided him, circling the nub at the top of her womanhood, the part which Scarlett had called the clitoris during their earlier lesson.

Kyra's breath quickened, heat flushing through her body, an insistent throb between her thighs. Her hands curled into fists, struggling to contain her reaction; she may have even moaned.

Jewell's breath grew short, her voice trembling. "Yes ... yes, right there ... faster."

"But we must never forget about the man," Scarlett said, and in response, Jewell licked the palm of her free hand, then reached down and gripped Bryan's manhood, stroking.

"Why did she lick her hand?" Kyra asked.

"For lubrication. It feels better to the man," Scarlett explained.

Bryan let out a loud groan. "Oh God!" he gasped, his voice high and strangled. A moment later his body jerked as liquid spilled from his member.

At the same time, Jewell cried out, her body shaking. "Yes. Yes! I'm there."

Kyra's core tightened, heat coursing through her as she watched the aftermath of their release. She stole a glance at Mr. Kent behind her. His jaw was tight, his hands strangling the small notebook in his lap, but his gaze was not on the couple by the bed. It was on Kyra.

"Are you all right, Mr. Kent?" Kyra reached out to him, concerned by his pained expression.

"I ..." He shot to his feet, moving briskly toward the door. "I must go. Thank you. Goodbye."

And for the second time that day, Mr. Kent made haste and fled, leaving Kyra in a whirlwind of confusion and curiosity.

8

DECLAN

Declan stormed down the hallway, hands awkwardly shielding the swelling in his trousers, boots clapping against the wooden floor as he made a beeline for his room.

His mind was a mess, filled with images he shouldn't have seen. Jewell and Bryan's enthusiasm had seared itself into his brain. And then there was Miss Bailey, standing there, her cheeks as pink as a prairie sunrise, and the little gasps and moans that escaped her parted lips as she watched. It had sent his blood rushing straight south.

He hadn't meant to look at her and watch her cheeks go rosy, her thighs tense through the thin material of her skirt, her eyes alight. She'd looked to be close to the edge herself, watching like that. And if she was anywhere near as worked up as he was... well, they were both in trouble.

His body begged for relief. Twice today he'd been caught in this hellfire, and twice he'd resisted the urge to take matters into his own hands—quite literally. But now, with the memory of Miss Bailey's flustered face mingled with her soft gasps, he couldn't hold back any longer.

He shoved into his room and slammed the door. No time for patience. His hands flew to the buttons of his trousers, and he sighed in relief as he freed himself, gripping his aching cock. A few rough strokes had his pulse racing.

Thunder and lightning, it felt good.

His head fell back as his hand moved faster, his heart speeding into a gallop with each stroke, needing it rougher than usual. What would it be like to feel a woman's touch, to hear those breathy moans up close?

His breath hitched as his body neared the breaking point, his hands working furiously, one massaging his taut balls while the other slid up and down his length, slick and hot. He groaned, his release moments away. God, he could hardly stand it. His hips trembled, his legs barely holding him up, as the energy swirled around his prick.

He was right there. Right at the edge. Yes! Yes, he was about to explo—

Knock, knock.

"Mr. Kent? Are you okay?" It was Miss Bailey's voice. The knob began to turn.

Declan's heart stopped, but his body didn't—he was already too far gone. Panic hit him like a stampede.

"No!" he choked, but it was too late. The door pushed open, and Miss Bailey walked in.

"Oh God!" he yelled as his release hit with brutal force, his body convulsing as his seed spurted, the last bit of control slipping from his grasp. "I can't stop!"

Miss Bailey gasped, her eyes wide as saucers, staring at him in all his glory as he rode out his climax right in front of her. His body jerked, horror and elation wrapped into one.

Miss Bailey gasped, backing into the door as if she could melt through it. "I—I'm so sorry, sir. So sorry!" She scrambled to find the handle, her fingers fumbling in a mad dash for escape. Finally, the door opened, and she stumbled out, gone.

Declan dropped to his knees, panting and spent, mortification setting in like a sharp slap. "Goddammit!" He banged his fists into the floorboards. How the hell could he look her in the eye ever again?

There was a chattering of voices in the hallway, and Declan shot up, tucking himself back into his trousers and locking the door with shaky hands. He leaned his forehead against the cool wood, willing the ground to swallow him whole.

THE NEXT MORNING, Declan still hadn't left his room. He'd spent the entire night in a fit, trying to figure out how to navigate this disaster. He couldn't leave, so there was only one solution. Miss Bailey had to go.

A sharp knock broke through his thoughts, and he swung the door open, ready to face whatever fresh hell awaited him.

"Good morning, Mr. Kent," Scarlett said. Declan studied her face, checking for any sign that Miss Bailey had spilled the humiliating incident from last night, but Scarlett stood there, her expression unreadable, though her voice carried its usual businesslike calm. Not a flicker of amusement.

"Where's Miss Bailey?" Declan asked, his voice a bit rougher than he intended.

"I asked her to collect the linens from the guest bedrooms and put them in the barrel out back to be washed. Would you like me to fetch her?"

"I need to speak with you about something," he began, jamming his feet into his boots and grabbing his hat. He'd been itching for a ride on his horse, Blaze.

"I can guess what it's about." Scarlett shifted the leather folder that she held in her hands. "I know you disapprove of my business, and seeing as you ran out on us last night, I thought you may be considering shutting us down. That's why I'm here. To show you some numbers."

Declan took the leather folder offered to him. He placed it on the desk against the windows.

"It's not about that. I want to speak to you about Miss Bailey. I don't want any more training or lessons for her. She's an unnecessary expense. We don't need another girl. It's time she leaves."

Scarlett crossed her arms and studied Declan. "Kyra stays. She's my niece, and she's got nowhere else to go."

"I don't ca—"

His protest was cut off as Scarlett, not one to mince words, continued, "Let me remind you, Mr. Kent, the Bluebonnet Belles bring in more coin than the hotel and saloon combined. If Kyra leaves, so do I, and my business goes with me."

Declan gritted his teeth. He knew Scarlett wasn't exaggerating. He didn't need to look at the books to see that the Belles were the backbone of this operation, although he would comb over all the accounts later and confirm it.

"Fine," Declan snapped. "She can stay. But not as a"—he gestured vaguely—"not as a Belle. She can work as a maid in the hotel. Whatever is needed."

"You're a virile man, Mr. Kent." Scarlett's lips curled into a sly smile. "Maybe what's bothering you is how much you like Miss Bailey." Declan glared, but Scarlett wasn't finished. "I doubt the feeling's mutual, so you may want to reconsider her coming under my tutelage. It might be your only chance to have her." She turned and swept out the door before Declan could respond, leaving him simmering with irritation and confusion.

What a silly woman. He had no interest in Miss Bailey. She was a beauty, yes, but he needed more than that if he were going to court a woman. He'd certainly never pay to be with Miss Bailey or any woman. No, the only thing he'd pay for would be to see her squirm with the same humiliation he'd suffered.

Yes, that would bring him great pleasure.

9

KYRA

yra's sleep had been erratic at best, haunted by what she'd witnessed. Images of Mr. Kent; his hand on himself, his groans rumbling through her mind, his release—violent and raw. And that look on his face when he'd realized she was standing there. Pure horror.

Her body had lit up like kindling near a roaring fire. She'd frozen, unable to tear her eyes away, overwhelmed by the pull in her belly, by the scandalous sight of him losing control.

Then there was the throbbing between her legs, the one that had started when she'd watched Jewell with Bryan. But after seeing *him*, the feeling had intensified tenfold. Her fingers had even twitched, itching to mimic what Jewell had done, to explore her own body as Scarlett had suggested.

Part of her knew she should try it out. As Scarlett had said, she needed to know what that climax felt like. But when her hand slid beneath her skirt in the dark of her room, she'd chickened out and curled up in the small bed and tried to think of anything but Mr. Kent—his broad, heaving chest, the way his mouth had fallen open as pleasure overtook him.

Everything about last night had awakened something foreign

inside her—a burning curiosity. Not just about Mr. Kent, but for herself. For knowledge. For the rush of that heated feeling.

And Jewell. Her body had been so different from Kyra's own —smaller breasts, those impossibly dark nipples that had been hard as pebbles. Even the hair between her legs was tighter, darker, curling close to her skin. Kyra's own was lighter, fairer, finer.

She shook her head, shaking these unencumbered thoughts from her mind. She'd chosen this life, chosen to be here and see these things, but she didn't realize how *strange* it would feel. Odd, but also exhilarating.

Oh, if Henry could see her now. Of course, he would probably be too drunk to see anything. Not that Henry had ever really seen her. When he had managed to lie with her, it was sloppy—unsatisfying. He'd cry afterward, then pass out in a heap, leaving Kyra to take the quilt and sleep on the kitchen floor just to escape his sweaty, stinking body.

The memories left a bitter taste in her mouth, and when the sun peeked over the horizon, she jumped out of bed, desperate to shake off the sticky thoughts of her past.

In the kitchen, she cut a slice of bread, took a peach from the icebox, and headed out onto the raised porch at the front of the hotel, nibbling at her breakfast and watching the sleepy town slowly come to life.

It was Sunday, and people were dressed in their finery heading to church. Kyra had never been a pious woman, but she liked the reverence of church and the sweet sounds of the hymns.

Scarlett called her in to fetch the linens, and Kyra dumped her plate in the kitchen and hurried to comply. After she finished her morning chores, Kyra slipped out the back, desperate for a walk to clear her mind. The sun played hide-and-seek with the clouds, its warmth a gentle balm.

At the end of Main Street, just before the road veered off, she spotted the stables. A blond Quarter Horse neighed softly from behind the fence, and she walked over and petted his nose.

Kyra loved to ride. She'd had to leave her horse, Luna, behind when she left, and only now did she realize how much she longed for the freedom of a good ride.

A black-and-white collie darted past her, chasing a stick. The dog raced toward a man near the stables, wagging its tail furiously. Kyra laughed at the sweet dog, but when she raised her eyes to the man, she froze.

Mr. Kent stood next to a large chestnut horse, cooing and treating it with the gentleness of a father. The dog nudged his leg, and Mr. Kent knelt, ruffling the dog's fur with a gentle smile, then tossed the stick again. It landed near her feet, and before she could retreat, his eyes found hers.

Memories of the night before rushed through her mind—Mr. Kent's powerful frame trembling, his face contorted with pleasure, lost to sensation. The strangled sounds that had escaped his throat, the way his control had fractured completely.

Again, her hands trembled with the urge to touch herself, to discover if she could find that same release.

The horse next to her bumped her arm, pulling her attention from her heated thoughts. When she looked back at Mr. Kent, he was leading his horse away from the stables, the dog skipping next to him like they were old friends.

For the first time, Kyra found herself wondering what else Mr. Kent had left behind in Kentucky. A farm? A family? Maybe a wife, or a sweetheart? The thought stirred something unpleasant in her chest, and she quickly brushed it aside.

She continued her walk, arriving at the small, whitewashed church. The final hymn drifted through the open door and she lingered on the steps, listening to the music with a small, wistful smile.

When the service was winding down, she walked across the road, not wanting to encounter any of the townsfolk. She doubted many of them would want to befriend her once they learned that she was to be a painted lady.

The door to the church opened wider, and a man stepped out —a tall, lean figure with thick, black hair and a badge glinting on his hip. His eyes, deep blue and sharp as a hawk's, locked on her as she passed.

"Wait one minute, miss."

Her heart jumped, and she quickened her pace, pretending she hadn't heard. But his boots were quick, and before she knew it, his hand had closed around her arm, gentle but firm.

"Miss," he said, his voice steady. "Slow your pace."

Kyra bit her lip, tamping down the irritation bubbling up inside her. "Apologies, sir. I'm in a hurry."

"You're Scarlett's new girl, aren't you?"

She kept her head bent, afraid of what this lawman might say or do. Scarlett had said the sheriff was a friend of the brothel, but Kyra didn't know if this was one of his deputies or the sheriff himself.

"I've no quarrel with that, if that's your worry," the man added, a smile crinkling the corners of his eyes.

Kyra blinked up at him, surprised by the warmth in his gaze.

"I was wondering ..." He hesitated, rubbing the back of his neck. "Would you mind if I spent some time with you tonight?"

"Oh." Kyra's eyebrows shot up. "I ... I haven't really started, er, working yet."

His eyes widened slightly, but he recovered quickly. "Is this your first time?"

"Yes." Kyra's face heated as she blurted the answer.

"Would you extend me the honor of being your first customer? I'll pay extra."

People started coming out of the church, and the lawman took hold of Kyra's arm. Not hard, but enough to move them away from prying eyes.

"What's your name?" Kyra asked, her voice softer now.

"Sheriff Mack." He tipped his hat back, his smile confident. "Ask Scarlett about me. I'm a good customer. Don't hit or hurt the girls."

A knot formed in Kyra's throat at his words. The fact that he felt the need to say it meant there were men who weren't so kind.

He took a step back, then paused, looking at her intently. "Wait, have you never ... at all?"

"Oh, um, I was married, but my husband is ... gone." She refrained from telling him that she was still technically married, or that the story she told everyone—that her husband had run out on her—wasn't entirely true. "That's why I came. Scarlett is my aunt."

"That's a relief." He smiled that charming smile again. "I didn't want to be the one to break you in."

He disappeared into the crowd, leaving Kyra standing alone, her heart racing. The weight of her new life pressed down on her. The sheriff had seemed kind enough, and suddenly she wanted to know what it would feel like to bring a man to the brink and watch him explode. All because of her.

Maybe Scarlett was right. Maybe there was power in this work. And maybe, just maybe, she might enjoy herself. Especially with a man like Sheriff Mack.

10

DECLAN

Blaze's hooves thundered against the packed earth, but after an hour of riding, Declan couldn't shake the shame that crawled through him after spotting Miss Bailey at the stables. It had all come flooding back—her standing in his doorway, the horrifying moment when his release had overtaken him, unable to stop even as she'd witnessed it.

Declan tried to shake her from his mind, but something lingered. The way she'd looked at him by the stables, her expression dark and hungry, made his blood run hot. It wasn't the disgust or mockery he'd expected, but a heat that made his skin prickle with awareness.

He tightened his grip on the reins, urging Blaze to gallop faster, fixing his mind on the road ahead and these new surroundings. Far away from Miss Bailey and the Bluebonnet Hotel.

Kentucky had rolling hills, green as far as the eye could see, and fertile land perfect for horses. Texas was a whole other beast —dry, flat, the creeks shriveling up in the heat, and the kind of plains that stretched endlessly, making a man feel lost even when he knew exactly where he was going.

The sun clung to his back and he slowed Blaze to a trot, steering him to the edge of a wooded area. They stopped under a large sycamore and he dismounted. Blaze snorted as Declan handed him one of the apples, chomping it down in no time. Declan leaned back against the shady tree, muscles pleasantly sore from the ride. He needed this—the open air, the quiet—anything to stop thinking about the mess waiting for him back in town.

He pulled out his beat-up pocket watch and checked the time. It wasn't even noon. If he continued, he could reach Frisco in the next few hours, and frankly, he itched to visit his brother. It had been over a week since he last heard from Clive, and with every day that passed, Declan's gut twisted tighter.

It had taken years, but Declan had a chunk of money saved. The plan had always been clear: save enough cash to buy a small ranch, get their mother out of debt, and give his sister an escape from her bastard of a husband. Declan had worked himself to the bone, saving every penny. But now, with Clive's neck on the line and the Bluebonnet Hotel weighing on his shoulders like a boulder, that dream was more distant than ever.

Declan pushed off from the tree, determination hardening his features. He mounted Blaze and took off toward Frisco, his mind already turning over the numbers, the plan taking shape as his horse pounded the ground beneath him.

Hours later, Declan dismounted and tied Blaze to the post outside the Frisco sheriff's office. He dusted himself off, took a sip from his canteen, and pushed into the building.

"Afternoon, Sheriff," Declan said, tipping his hat to the broad man sitting behind a solid oak desk. Sheriff Adler stood, brushing his light brown hair under his Stetson, his skin a deep brown from the harsh Texas sun. "I'm Declan Kent. I'm here to see my brother."

The sheriff gave him a long, assessing look before jerking his head toward the back of the building where Declan assumed Clive was being held. "He shot my deputy, ya know?"

Declan halted. "Clive said it was an accident."

"Yeah." The sheriff narrowed his gaze, but there was a spark of amusement. "He was aiming for me."

In the back room, they passed a few cells, and Sheriff Adler finally stopped in front of one, resting a hand on the iron bars. Declan stepped up to the dim cell where Clive was being kept, his brother sprawled on a straw mattress staring at the ceiling. Clive's face lit up the second he saw Declan.

"Brother!" Clive rushed to the bars.

Declan met him, their hands clasping tightly in fists around the bars. "You shot a deputy?"

"Nah, I was aiming for him." Clive pointed to the sheriff, and the two shared a smile, as if they were in on a joke. "He knows I wouldn't have really shot him. But his deputy was eager to show off and got in the way."

Declan wiped his brow with the bandana from around his neck, the spring heat unrelenting in the stuffy jail.

"What in the hell were you thinking?" Declan asked.

"Ah, it wasn't serious. Some folks at the bar were piling hats on the sheriff's head. Bet me I couldn't shoot the top one off."

"So, you did shoot at the sheriff." Declan glanced at the sheriff, who raised an eyebrow but said nothing.

"At the hats."

Declan turned to Sheriff Adler. "Is that true?"

"Don't know. Didn't see nothin'," the sheriff drawled wryly. "But my deputy was sitting behind me, got a little excited, and caught the bullet in his shoulder."

"It sounds like an accident. Can't you let him go?"

Sheriff Adler unlocked the cell, escorting Clive to a table by the window and handcuffing him to a bar. "The law's the law. There were a lot of witnesses, and Deputy Eli's family insisted on pressing charges. So here we are. Holler when you're done."

As the sheriff walked away, Clive sat back, grinning as if he'd won the lottery. "I knew you'd come, Deck. You always do."

"Clive, this isn't a damn joke. You may be chummy with the sheriff, but it's gonna be up to a jury whether or not you hang for this."

"They won't convict me. It was an accident." Clive tipped his chin up toward the window, sniffing the fresh air through the cracked pane. "Besides, I was doing business for the saloon."

Declan didn't ask what kind of business. He knew better than to poke *that* hornet's nest. "Is your lawyer as confident as you?"

"I got rid of the lawyer."

"Damn it, Clive," Declan muttered. "You always find a way to make things harder. I'm gonna have to sell the saloon, and we need to find you another lawyer."

"You can't sell it." Clive's eyes widened, panic finally setting in. "I signed it over to you so the law couldn't take it away from me."

"You've painted us into a corner." Declan's shoulders sank. He should've known his little brother wouldn't understand the gravity of his situation. "This time you really screwed up." Declan stood and shoved his hat on his head.

"Please don't do this," Clive begged.

Declan exhaled deeply. "I didn't do this. You did. Even with all my savings and selling the saloon, it still won't guarantee your freedom. But it's your best chance."

His brother may hate him for it, but Declan had to sell the hotel. And he had to sell it fast.

11

KYRA

Kyra toyed with the rim of her supper bowl, her fingers tracing the edge as she sat cross-legged on the empty stage beside Mei and Jewell. The three women dug into their noodles and chicken, fueling up before the inevitable chaos of the night. The saloon was starting to hum with energy, and Kyra could already feel the thrum of excitement in the air.

Her gaze darted between her companions as she chewed, her mind racing back to her encounters with Mr. Kent that morning and then, much to her dismay, with the sheriff right outside the church.

"What do you know about Sheriff Mack?" she asked, trying to sound casual, though her stomach churned.

"Why?" Mei asked, wiping a droplet of broth from her chin.

"He said he wants to be my first customer," Kyra said. Jewell and Mei exchanged a look, and Kyra's belly flipped. "What? Is he bad?"

A little laugh escaped Mei's lips that she quickly stopped. "No. He's just ... particular," she said, but her voice held a teasing tone.

Particular. That didn't exactly put Kyra at ease. She glanced at

Jewell, hoping for more clarity, but her friend was busy wiping her fingers clean, looking far too amused for Kyra's comfort.

"You're scaring her," Jewell said, playfully batting at Mei's shoulder.

"He likes you to be in control," Mei said, tucking the bottom hem of her royal-blue skirt into her waistband, exposing her leg —an act that would be shocking anywhere but here.

Kyra put her bowl down, no longer hungry. "In control of what? I don't know how this works."

"None of us did at first," Jewell said, offering a softer smile. "You'll learn as you go. Dive in, don't overthink it. And don't worry, Sheriff Mack isn't looking to hurt you."

That eased some of the tension coiled in Kyra's chest, but the knot in her stomach remained.

"But you'll need to wear something else. Your clothes are much too proper for a lady of the night," Mei said, standing up and swishing her hips, her stockings and pantaloons exposed in a manner that still made Kyra blink.

"The sheriff isn't fussy about appearances," Jewell said, gathering the dishes. "You'll be fine in just your chemise."

Mei took hold of Kyra's forearm, drawing her attention. "The sheriff's requests may seem unusual, but once you get used to it, it's fun. He's one of my favorite clients."

The saloon doors swung open, and Scarlett strode in, a woman on a mission. "Jewell, Mei, upstairs with you. Finish getting ready," she ordered, her tone firm but kind.

Kyra made to follow, but Scarlett caught her arm, holding her back. "Not you, Kyra. We need to talk."

Scarlett led the way to the small office behind the bar. Kyra hesitated outside the door. "Is Mr. Kent in there?"

Scarlett waved her off with a dismissive flick of the wrist. "No, he sent word he'll be in Frisco until late tonight. Something about his brother." Scarlett glanced down at the note she'd pulled from her pocket, her expression shifting. "Jonathan Mackenzie requested your services for tonight."

"Who's that?" Kyra asked, her belly tightening.

"The sheriff. He said he spoke to you this morning."

"Oh, Sheriff Mack. Yes."

"I told him you weren't ready," Scarlett said, her eyes gleaming with amusement, "but that made him even more interested. And I don't make it a habit to turn him down. He's the reason this place runs smoothly, keeping it safe for all my girls."

If this was going to be Kyra's new life, there was no point in backing down now. She straightened her shoulders. "I don't want you to treat me differently from any other new girl. I'll do it if that's his wish."

Scarlett tapped her nail on the folded paper in her hand. "There's one snag."

Kyra straightened, anxiety bubbling in her chest. "What is it?"

"Mr. Kent," Scarlett said slowly, "made it very clear that he doesn't want you working as one of my girls."

"He can't do that!" Kyra shouted, heat shooting up her neck.

"Technically, he can. But what he doesn't know can't hurt him. I hate to rush this, but it's best if you finish your session with the sheriff before Mr. Kent returns." Scarlett folded her hands in front of her lap. "The sheriff is already here, waiting, but we have a few minutes if you have any questions."

"I have a hundred," Kyra blurted out.

Scarlett smiled sympathetically. "Start with one."

"Mei said the sheriff likes the girls to be in control. I've only ever been with one man, and it was ... well, nothing like what I saw Jewell do with Bryan last night."

Scarlett's expression didn't waver, though a hint of understanding flickered in her eyes. "The sheriff will show you what he enjoys, and then he'll hand over the reins. It's not as daunting as it seems, Kyra. He knows you're new."

That didn't exactly settle Kyra's nerves, but Scarlett's confidence grounded her. "If you're not sure," Scarlett continued, her tone soft but firm, "this is the moment to walk away. No one's forcing your hand."

An image of Henry, stumbling through their door, drunk and bitter, flashed in Kyra's mind. The suffocating loneliness, the whispered rumors about his affairs with his students at Bates College, and the humiliation she endured for years bubbled up inside her. Her husband had been a cold, miserable man who blamed her for every misfortune. He may not have hit her, but his words had cut just as deeply.

No, Kyra wouldn't walk away. This was why she'd come here.

"Kyra." Scarlett took her hand. "Is this what you want?"

Kyra squeezed her aunt's hand in reassurance. "Yes. I won't go back to being that empty woman I was."

She'd been walking around as a shell of a woman for years. Being around these strong young ladies, still in service to men but also having some control of their lives, was intoxicating.

Kyra turned, her hands fumbling with the buttons of her dress. "Unbutton me, Aunt Scarlett. I've got a sheriff waiting, and I won't waste another minute of my life looking back."

1 2

KYRA

"**K**eep your underclothes on."

Sheriff Mack's low, rumbling voice filled the room, thick with command. He leaned casually against the tall dresser in Kyra's room, his bare chest and muscled abdomen glistening in the lamplight, already stripped down to his brown canvas trousers. He was a man carved from raw strength, and Kyra couldn't help but let her eyes wander over his form, appreciating the view. Rarely had she been able to indulge in its finery—not like this.

Under the thin fabric of her flimsy chemise, her heart pitter-pattered, nerves and excitement making her lightheaded. This moment, this night, was a step into a freedom she'd long craved. She'd waited years to find respite away from her horrid marriage, and this was her final step.

Sheriff Mack's eyes, dark and unreadable, were fixed on her, sending electric sparks down her spine. "What happens here, stays here," he said, his voice steady but intense. "Do you understand?"

Kyra nodded, her heartbeat so rapid she worried she'd pass out, but she breathed deeply, hoping the sheriff wouldn't notice

58

the tremble in her hands. Mei said he wouldn't hurt her, but there were many ways to injure someone that didn't include bodily harm.

"Kyra?" he pressed.

"I understand."

His lips twitched as if suppressing a grin. "My days are spent in control, running this town, making sure folks behave. In here, though ..." He let the sentence hang in the air, the implication clear. Still, he made certain she understood. "I don't want to think."

Kyra swallowed hard, stepping closer, feeling the heat radiating off his skin.

"This is your first time, correct?" The sheriff brushed a loose strand of Kyra's hair from her cheek, making her shiver. "As a Belle."

"Yes. I've been with my husband of course but, um ... it was ..." Kyra trailed off, embarrassed to speak the words.

"How did you bed him?" He unhooked his gun belt and dropped it on the vanity table with a clunk.

"I imagine how most people do."

"Be specific," he said, irritation in his voice.

Kyra's face flushed. She didn't want to relive those awkward nights with Henry, but she knew the sheriff expected an answer. "He climbed on top of me. He ... did what men do, and then it was over."

"No variety?"

Kyra shook her head. There had never been room for anything more with Henry. She'd learned to be still, to let him take what he wanted, and then disappear afterward.

"Come here." He tugged at the loose fabric of her chemise and pulled her closer so she brushed against his bare skin.

"I'll guide you at first," he said, his voice low. "And when you're comfortable, take control, commanding me."

"Oh." Kyra blinked, caught off guard. "What types of things shall I demand?"

"To start, tell me to take off my trousers."

This was new territory. Kyra had spent her life obeying commands, being told what to do, how to act. *As a woman does.* But now, in this room, with this man, the roles were reversing. And it intrigued her.

Her mind flashed back to training Luna, her spirited mare. To gain control of Luna, she'd had to be firm, show her who was in charge. This was no different. Well, maybe a little different.

There was no riding crop in her room, but she spotted the sterling silver paddle brush on the vanity. Without hesitation, she picked it up, slapping it lightly against her palm, testing the weight. A surge of confidence rushed through her.

"Take your pants off," she said, her voice gaining strength. "Now."

Sheriff Mack raised an eyebrow, his lip cocking up on one side as if he was laughing at her. Irritation rushed through her veins. Kyra brought the brush down hard against the vanity with a sharp crack, the sound reverberating through the room. His eyes widened, and without further delay, he unbuttoned his trousers and let them fall to the floor.

"And your drawers," Kyra said, gaining confidence.

He yanked at the drawstrings, and the long cotton pants fell on top of his trousers. Kyra kept her eyes on the clothing items, her earlier anxiety swirling in her chest, afraid to look at what was between his legs, knowing what came next.

"Kick them away," Kyra said, swallowing over her jitters.

He hesitated for a fraction of a second, and she responded by smacking her palm with the back of the brush again. His eyes darkened with heat as he nudged the clothes aside with his foot.

"This excites you?" Kyra asked, genuinely curious.

"Very much," he said, his chest rising and falling rapidly.

It was strange—this dynamic, this control. But also exhilarating. And she liked it. Even though it was only a charade. He had all the true power.

"Get on the bed," Kyra said, her mind spinning, thinking what she might demand next.

He shook his head, his voice dropping. "No. Tell me to get on all fours. Like an animal."

The brush fell from her hand, landing hard on his foot. "Oh God, I'm sorry." She quickly scooped it up.

"Don't ever apologize," he snapped.

Kyra's jaw dropped, but she quickly recovered, gripping the brush tighter. It was an odd request, but she complied. She had to. "On your knees, mongrel," she demanded, her voice firmer now.

Still, he didn't move. Was he testing her? She wasn't sure what else to say. Then Henry's face flashed across her mind—her awful husband, the man who had treated her like she was less than nothing. Rage ignited inside her.

"Then I'll make you." Before she could think twice, she grabbed Sheriff Mack by the ear and yanked. "I said on your knees!"

He gasped and sank to the floor, upright on his knees. Kyra's gaze clamped onto the taut length of his manhood lifting away from the dark tufts of hair surrounding it, hard and eager.

She twisted his ear again and he moaned from both pain and pleasure. A thrill shot through her. So pain excited him.

Still thinking of Henry, she raised the brush, and with only a moment of hesitation, she brought it down on his buttocks. Not hard, but enough to leave a mark.

He groaned, his body trembling under her command. His eyes met hers, and Kyra saw the spark of lust there, raw and unfiltered, and she knew her gamble had paid off. This was what he wanted.

"Touch it," she ordered, surprising even herself with how the words rolled off her tongue.

"What?" His hooded eyes glanced at her, momentarily confused.

She smacked him with the brush, and he moaned in pleasure, a droplet of liquid dripping from his tip.

"You heard me. Stroke yourself." She raised the brush in threat.

His gaze narrowed, and she worried she'd gone too far, but he obeyed, his hand wrapping around his manhood, stroking from base to tip.

She bit her lip, shocked and delighted by this game. How were these words coming out of her mouth?

Sheriff Mack's eyes rolled back as his right hand pumped fiercely. His left hand squeezed the solid muscle of his outer thigh subconsciously. Slowly his fingers moved around his hip to his buttocks, his thumb caressing the crease.

Kyra's breath quickened, enthralled by the power she held in this moment. The brush was heavy in her hand, but it was more than just an object—it was a symbol of something she hadn't realized she wanted until now. Control.

"Bend over. On your hands and knees," she said, her voice steady, "like a dog, and keep stroking."

Sheriff Mack obeyed, his body a mass of hard muscle as he followed her every word. He supported himself with his left hand as his right continued to fondle his manhood. Kyra smacked his backside with the brush. He grunted with each wallop. Suddenly, the brush slipped and the long end slid into his crack.

"Yes," he cried out. "Keep it there."

Kyra pulled back, looking at the brush curiously.

"Put it back," he growled, glancing over his shoulder.

"I give the orders," she said hastily, covering her uncertainty at what just happened. The end of the brush had entered his back-side, and he'd liked it.

Kyra took the handle of the brush and pushed it inside him

and watched in amazement as he writhed with pleasure. She sank the handle in further and his head snapped back on a loud moan.

"Deeper," he howled, his right hand pumping his member, his buttocks clenching around the brush handle.

Kyra moved the brush handle farther inside him, perplexed but following his command. He groaned, his face screwed up, lost in the pleasure he gave himself as well as the sensation he received from the end of the brush pressing into him.

"Oh Jesus, it's happening." His hand pumped faster, his hips rocking in rhythm with Kyra's movements. "Oh God. Yes, Kyra! Deeper! Yes!"

Kyra edged the brush handle in a little more and the sheriff roared. His hips trembled and liquid pumped from his member, his seed hitting the floor in spurts as his climax overtook him.

When his hips stopped trembling, Kyra slid the brush out and knelt behind him, her body flushed as with a fever, her breathing nearly as heavy as his. Soon his rapid breaths tapered, and the sheriff stood and began to dress.

Kyra stayed on the floor, looking up at him, until he buckled his holster and gun in place and walked to the door. He glanced over his shoulder and swiped a dark strand of hair from his forehead. "You're a pearl, Kyra. I shall request you again." The door shut with a click.

Kyra dropped the brush, a shocked laugh popping from her lips. She was bewildered by what had just happened, but more than that, she was elated.

Her dream was no longer in the distance. It had all become a reality—her new life, her power, and her freedom.

13

DECLAN

eclan had chased the sun all the way back from Frisco, riding Blaze hard, hoping the fast pace would wear away the fury that had been building in his chest since the moment he left the town to return to Wylde. But no amount of galloping quenched the fire burning in him.

By the time he arrived at the Bluebonnet Hotel, night had fully descended, the stars overhead offering little solace. Blaze had earned himself extra carrots for the journey, and Declan settled him into the stable before heading inside the hotel, hoping for some telegrams regarding the sale.

It had been several days since he'd sent word about the sale. Surely there would be some interest soon. In the meantime, he'd have to focus on whipping the place into shape—and fast.

He stepped into the saloon, where the noise of piano music and drunken laughter immediately assaulted his senses. The women were on stage, their skirts flying, kicking their legs in high arcs that had the men hollering and throwing coins.

And there, in the middle of it all, was Miss Bailey, kicking her legs and shaking her hips. The hot fury he'd hoped a half day's ride would leech from him fired up as soon as he looked upon her. He spun away from the stage, fearing he'd rush the platform and yank her off it if he continued to watch her prance about.

He clenched his fists at his sides, determined not to lose his temper in front of everyone. He scanned the room for Scarlett. There were many things they needed to discuss, including what the hell Miss Bailey was doing on that stage. He'd told Scarlett that Miss Bailey was not to be part of this circus. But before he could find her, his gaze landed on a man leaning against the bar, watching the stage intently—a man with a badge at his hip.

The sheriff of Wylde.

Declan's jaw tightened as he approached. "Evening, officer," he said, sliding his hat onto the bar beside the sheriff's. "Name's Declan Kent."

"I know who you are. I'm Sheriff Mackenzie, but everyone calls me Mack." He didn't bother tearing his eyes from the stage, where Miss Bailey's legs were still flashing. "Heard you were here. How's your brother?"

"Alive—for now. You know the sheriff in Frisco?"

Mack turned to him, his tanned skin crinkling with an amused smile. "Adler, sure. We used to drive cattle when we were younger men. I heard Clive tried to shoot him."

Declan snorted. "In a manner of speaking."

"Sheriff Adler's fair. None of that Wild West bullshit," Mack said, his eyes flicking back to the stage.

"It's not the sheriff I'm worried about." Declan's eyes narrowed toward the stage. "I hear you take care of these women. Shield them from harm?"

Mack slid his gaze back to Declan. "I'm no saint, Kent. But I make sure the ladies here are well taken care of, and I'm rewarded for my protection."

"Some men would take those rewards without offering anything in return," Declan pointed out.

"I have special tastes, and the gratitude of these women goes a long way." Mack smiled slowly, then glanced at the corner of the stage where Miss Bailey paid close attention to one of the patrons. "You've done well with the new girl. I had a taste of her earlier tonight, and she's going to be very good for business."

Anger twisted in Declan's gut. What the hell was Mack talking about? Declan had made it explicitly clear that Miss Bailey was to keep her legs shut.

Sheriff Mack slid his hat on his head and tipped the brim toward Declan's raggedy hat on the bar. "Go to the general store tomorrow. Betsy will sort out a proper hat for you."

"You're back," Bryan said and pushed a short glass of rum across the bar to the sheriff and him. Declan kept the glass on the bar, not partaking. He wanted his wits about him.

"Where's Scarlett?" Declan asked shortly. He'd witnessed this young man in a very vulnerable state, and Declan didn't want to engage in small talk.

"Not sure," Bryan said, moving over to a posse of cowboys who were eager for drinks.

There was a commotion at the stage. Several men, lousy on drink, plucked at the girls' skirts and groped their legs.

"Let me go!" Miss Bailey kicked at the man who held the hem of her skirt, and her heel made contact with his chin. The man howled and leaped toward her.

Declan rushed to the fight, faster than the sheriff. He barreled through the crowd, tossing one of the men aside like a rag doll. The sheriff and Lorenzo wrestled the others out the door, while Declan snatched Miss Bailey.

Wild-eyed and flushed, she fought him as he grabbed her by the arm, hauling her off the stage before she could cause any more of a scene. "Let go of me!" she spat, kicking and wriggling in his grip.

Declan dragged her up the stairs, his pulse hammering in his throat, and threw open the door to her room before shoving her inside.

She spun on him like a fury, her palm cracking against his cheek. "How dare you!"

"Control yourself, woman!" Declan snarled, rubbing his stinging cheek. "What the hell were you doing down there? I told Scarlett you're not to be part of the bawdy entertainment!"

Miss Bailey flung her palms out and shoved his chest. "I can do whatever I damn well please!"

Declan's eyes blazed with fury, taking a dangerous step toward her. Miss Bailey stepped back, a touch of fear crossing her features. He spoke, his voice low and tight. "I own this place, which means nothing you do here is done without my approval. Including whoring."

Her chest heaved, eyes glinting with a mix of fear and something darker. "What is it, Mr. Kent? Afraid of a woman knowing her own mind? Or maybe you're afraid of something else." She raised a brow, her voice turning sultry, mocking. "Have you ever had a woman tame your beast?"

"How dare you!" Declan lunged forward and snatched her shoulders. "I should toss you out with the rubbish. You're lucky I've allowed you to stay after ... after everything."

Her gray eyes darkened nearly to coal. "That's it, isn't it? All this fury because you can't handle the fact that these women know more about giving pleasure to a lady than you do."

Declan's jaw muscles ticked, his control hanging by a thread as she leaned closer, her finger trailing along the waistband of his trousers. His body betrayed him, heat pooling low in his gut. Declan gripped her wrist, yanking her hand away.

"Enough," he growled, but even he could hear the unsteady edge to his voice. He needed to get out of here. Now.

With a quick twist, he pulled the master key from his pocket. "You'll stay in here until you learn some respect. Or I'll throw your smart mouth on the street."

She wrenched out of his grip and turned to him, resting her

palm against his chest. His heart beat like a hammer, momentarily under her spell.

Miss Bailey glanced up at Declan, her eyes so close he could see black specks in her pupils. "I'm right, aren't I? The beast in your pants has never been tamed by anything but your hand." She tilted her chin up and whispered, "I can help with that."

Miss Bailey's breasts tickled his chest, her finger sliding down, caressing his stomach. Lust filled his groin, and Declan fought every instinct to cover his arousal, which was on full display. "I don't need help."

"You need taming," she said pointedly toward his crotch, but the steam had left her words, leaving a tremble in her voice.

"I can tame myself," he growled.

"I'm aware." She smiled slyly, and Declan wanted to tear the look from her pretty face. Instead, he held up the master key and sauntered to the door, clicking it into the keyhole.

"What are you doing?" She rushed toward him, eyes wide. "You can't lock me in here!"

Declan yanked the door shut and turned the lock, pocketing the key. "I can do whatever I damn well please, Miss Bailey. I'm your boss."

14

KYRA

Kyra paced, the floorboards in her room creaking under her step, her thoughts spinning wildly. She'd finally claimed her new life and, just like that, Mr. Kent had ripped it from her grasp.

Blast that man!

Her fists were red and sore from pounding on the locked door. No one had heard her. Of course not. The only rooms at this end of the hall were her own and Mr. Kent's, and he certainly wasn't about to come to her rescue.

Kyra slumped into the small chair by the window, her gaze moving toward the bustling street below. The gas lamps flickered as shadows moved across the dirt road, and she strained to see anyone she might know.

She cursed under her breath, frustration burning in her chest. She'd thought she had figured out how to wield the power Scarlett and the other women did so effortlessly. They could bend men to their will with just a glance, a touch, a whisper. And yet, everything she did infuriated Mr. Kent.

She doubted she could seduce him even if she wanted to. Either Mr. Kent had zero attraction to her, or he was a very good actor. If the former was true, then his prick had a mind of its own, as it had certainly responded. The rest of him was as rigid as a boulder.

Kyra sighed, her head falling back against the chair. Questioning his virginity had been a mistake. She hadn't just pushed the wrong button; she'd ignited a full-blown explosion. He'd looked ready to throttle her. They say you get more flies with honey, but she'd tried both sweetness and poison, and neither had worked.

What was the key to unlocking Mr. Kent ... and her door?

The sheriff had taken a liking to her. He'd watched her all evening as she pranced around the stage, showing off the dances she'd learned that day. If the sheriff wanted her, surely Mr. Kent would have no choice but to let her work.

Kyra's gaze drifted back to the street. She kept vigil at the window for the next hour, watching the world move on without her, her impatience growing like a weed in her chest. Then finally, she spotted Mei outside, enticing the passersby with her smile and a swish of her skirts. Kyra banged on the windowpane, but the din of the street drowned out her attempts at grabbing Mei's attention.

Kyra pried at the window's edge with her short nails, trying to loosen its rusty hinges. Was she to be in here all night? Or longer?

None of her attempts to escape worked, and by the following afternoon, her stomach growled in hunger. She twisted her sore hands in her lap where she sat at her vanity, bored and furious. She'd pounded the door half the day, but her hands were too raw to continue.

In the hall, there were voices. Kyra shot up from the chair and scrambled to the door, pressing her ear against the wood. Her heart leapt when she recognized one of them.

"Scarlett!" she hollered, her palm banging the door. "Scarlett, help!"

"Kyra?" The door handle shook. Scarlett's muffled voice was filled with concern. "Why is this locked?"

Before Kyra could answer, Mr. Kent's low, rumbling voice spoke outside the door, thick with irritation. After a brief argument—too quiet for her to make out clearly—the lock clicked, and the door swung open, revealing Scarlett holding a key.

"Are you alright?" Scarlett asked, concern flashing across her face.

Kyra's eyes shot to Mr. Kent, standing just behind Scarlett, his expression as hard as stone. Fury burned in her chest all over again. "Keep him away from me, or I swear I'll scratch his eyes out!"

Kyra lunged forward, but Scarlett quickly held her back, giving Mr. Kent a warning glare.

"How long have you been in here?" Scarlett asked.

"Since last night," Kyra huffed.

"If you ever lock her in again," Scarlett said, her voice low and dangerous, "I'll take all my girls and walk out of this place."

Mr. Kent's jaw tightened, his voice cold as he replied, "Then go. I won't stop you."

Scarlett's eyes narrowed. "The sheriff won't be pleased. And if you displease him, you'll never get the sale of this place through."

"He has no say in it," Mr. Kent bit back.

"He has *all* the say in this town." Scarlett released Kyra but stayed between her and Mr. Kent.

"He's taken a liking to Kyra, but she needs more practice. We wouldn't want another mishap like that unfortunate business with the girl who thought Mack's prick was a chew toy." Scarlett turned to Kyra, her voice gentler. "Teeth are to be used sparingly when putting a man into your mouth. As in, not at all."

"This isn't the time for lessons," Mr. Kent said sharply.

"I'll only say this one more time, Mr. Kent. Kyra is staying, and she'll continue her instructions. In fact, she'll continue them right now. Whether you like it or not. I know you're desperate to help your brother, and I know his trial is looking dire. I'd suggest you not make enemies here."

Mr. Kent's nostrils flared, but he did not argue. "Do what you wish. But no free rides for the johns. And I need Bryan and the other barkeep working in the saloon."

Scarlett, ever the provocateur, reached up and traced a finger down Mr. Kent's cheek, her thumb teasing at his bottom lip, tugging it open. "What about you, Mr. Kent? Would you like to have your cock suckled?"

Mr. Kent whacked her hand away, his expression a mixture of shock and indignation. "Absolutely not."

Scarlett laughed and then called out through the open door, "Enzo!"

Heavy footfalls made their way down the hall, and Lorenzo poked his head into the room. "Everything alright, ma'am?"

"Peachy. Can you ask Jacob to come up to Kyra's room in thirty minutes?" Scarlett dismissed him and then turned to Kyra. "We need to finish your instructions with haste, dear. The sheriff is expecting perfection. Go grab a quick bite and then freshen up. Once you're ready, meet me back here. If you're up for it?"

Kyra shot a hateful glare at Mr. Kent. "Oh, I'm ready. And nothing will stop me this time."

A short while later, Kyra was fresh as a rose, her stomach happily filled. Standing in the room that had imprisoned her all day, she didn't know what to expect from this night's adventure.

Scarlett nudged Kyra around and untied the laces of her corset with practiced fingers. "You don't want to be tied up like a hog when you're giving a man his pleasures."

Mr. Kent, who insisted on being there, leaned against the wall, his arms folded across his chest, scowling at the women. Kyra, still enraged by how he'd locked her up, preferred him gone, but Scarlett said he had a right to witness his employees in action.

Kyra's stomach twisted into knots as Scarlett worked the fabric loose, anticipating what the night might hold. Then, a tall, dark-skinned man with striking indigo eyes stepped into the room. He was younger than Kyra by a few years and handsome in a way that made her heart skip.

"Jacob," Scarlett purred. "So good of you to join us."

"Evening, ma'am," Jacob said with a slow, Southern drawl.

"Young man, I don't suppose you'd mind if Kyra gives your flute a play?"

Mr. Kent's face flushed a furious crimson. "For God's sake, woman, have some decency."

This sent Scarlett into a fit of giggles. "Decency is exactly what we don't want in a whorehouse."

Jacob, meanwhile, looked a bit unsure, his gaze flicking nervously to Mr. Kent, who stood stiff as a board near the door.

"Who are you? What do you do here?" Mr. Kent asked.

"He's our new security man for the girls, but he doesn't start until next week," Scarlett told Mr. Kent. "He's shadowing Enzo until he officially begins his duties. Any other objections?"

"Too many to list," Mr. Kent grumbled.

Scarlett ignored him. "There's a cloth and bowl of water on the table there, Jacob. Use it to wash your stick and berries and then lie on the bed."

Jacob followed her instructions, and soon his naked form lay sprawled on the bed before Kyra. His member, still soft, rested against his thigh, and Kyra couldn't help but stare. How on earth was she supposed to bring it to life?

"Use this." Scarlett pulled a small pot from her skirt pocket. "It's cream. Rub some on your palms and fingers."

"You gonna watch the whole time, sir?" Jacob asked Mr. Kent, who still hovered by the door.

"It's my job to know everything happening in this place." Mr.

Kent leaned casually against the frame of the open door, but the tic in his jaw gave away his discomfort.

"Gently take him in your hand and stroke upward with slight pressure," Scarlett instructed.

Kyra obeyed, her fingers slick with cream as she knelt beside Jacob. The skin of his member was warm, softer than she expected. She stroked gently, glancing up at Scarlett every few seconds. "Nothing's happening," Kyra whispered, her voice tight with anxiety.

"Don't look at me," Scarlett said. "Ask him what he likes."

Kyra swallowed her nerves. "Am I doing something wrong?"

Jacob shrugged, looking entirely too relaxed for a man in his position. "Not really. It's just strange with a man watching." His eyes flicked to Mr. Kent, who hadn't moved from his post by the door.

Kyra continued for another few minutes with no thickening of his member. "Do you want me to stop?"

"Probably best." Jacob swung his long legs to the side of the bed, yanked on his undergarment and trousers, and smiled brightly. "I sure do appreciate the effort."

Despite the failed attempt, Jacob left the room with a bounce in his step, his easygoing nature untouched by the awkward experience. Utterly defeated, Kyra sulked on the bed. "What did I do wrong?"

Scarlett patted her shoulder. "Nothing, darling. Sometimes a man's sausage just doesn't want to be tenderized." Scarlett handed Kyra a handkerchief to wipe her hands.

Lorenzo stepped into the doorway next to Mr. Kent. "Ma'am, the sheriff would like a moment."

Sheriff Mack strolled into the room, his broad smile flashing beneath the wide brim of his Stetson. "Evening, ladies." He tipped his hat. "I'm eager to make an appointment with Miss Kyra. When will she be ready?"

Kyra bit the inside of her cheek, remembering the things she'd done to him with her hairbrush. It was titillating and strange all at once. He must want more than that if he asked Scarlett to continue her training.

"Not quite." Scarlett placed her hand in the crook of Mack's elbow. "We are lacking a male volunteer to help Miss Kyra in her studies."

Mack's gaze slid lazily around the room, landing on Mr. Kent. His arms were crossed, his expression stony, but Kyra didn't miss the tightening of his jaw or the flicker of discomfort in his eyes.

"Why don't you use him?" Mack drawled, his grin widening as if he were suggesting the most innocent of solutions.

Kyra's heart leapt into her throat, and she opened her mouth to object, but Scarlett spoke first.

"What a wonderful idea," Scarlett said with a dazzling smile.

Mr. Kent stood as still as a statue, but the corded muscles of his neck were taut, his fists clenched at his sides. He said nothing, but his silence screamed louder than any protest.

"Yes, very clever." Kyra forced a smile.

"What do you say, Declan?" The sheriff raised his eyebrows.

"I say not on my mother's life," Mr. Kent snapped.

The sheriff's gaze darkened to black. "I'd be careful saying no to me, Mr. Kent. Sheriff Adler's practically my kin, and we wouldn't want anything to disrupt your brother's trial."

Mr. Kent seethed with anger, giving Kyra hope that this insanity would stop here.

"Then, of course, Sheriff," Mr. Kent said through gritted teeth. "Anything to help."

The sheriff chuckled. He might think he liked to give over control, but he was clearly getting off on controlling Mr. Kent's sexual fate.

"This should be fun," Sheriff Mack said, smiling wickedly, confirming Kyra's suspicions. "I look forward to discovering what you learn."

He sauntered out, leaving a silence so thick it practically

echoed. Kyra's skin felt too tight, her pulse pounding in her ears as she tried to process what had just happened.

Scarlett clapped her hands once, and Kyra flinched, her nerves raw with anticipation. "You two heard the man. Let's not waste any time. Snap to it."

Mr. Kent glowered, his molten eyes locking on Kyra, furious enough to tear the whole hotel down around them. How could he be angry at her? She hadn't demanded this of him.

"How can I give pleasure to a man who despises me?" Kyra asked.

"Hate can be quite the aphrodisiac, darling." Scarlett tilted her head, her eyes gleaming. "Consider it a lesson in what I like to call sex and loathing."

Mr. Kent stepped forward, his boots thudding ominously against the wooden floor. His gaze never left Kyra's, and for a moment, Kyra wondered if he'd refuse and storm out.

But instead, he stopped just short of her, his voice a low, dangerous rumble. "Let's get this over with."

Kyra's pulse roared in her ears, but she held her ground, meeting his fiery gaze with a spark of her own. "With pleasure," she said sarcastically, a sharp edge in her voice.

It wasn't just a challenge—it was a war waiting to be fought. And neither of them would surrender.

15

DECLAN

This was outrageous. Declan had never been touched by a woman, and he didn't want his first time to be with a prostitute-in-training. He'd been raised proper, after all. He always presumed his first experience would be with his wife, not a woman who was practically being coerced to be with him. But here he stood, in the middle of Miss Bailey's room, caught between duty and desire.

He didn't begrudge these working women their fight for freedom and autonomy in a world that often crushed them. No, he'd seen firsthand what that looked like—mending the bruises and welts his sister had endured at the hands of her cruel husband.

That thought alone spurred him forward. He needed the sheriff on his side if he had any hope of rescuing his sister and saving his brother from hanging by a rope. He had to play along.

"You're willing to go forth with this insanity?" Miss Bailey asked again, standing before him.

"Do I have a choice?" Declan grumbled.

"I shall not force you," Miss Bailey said, crossing her arms over her chest like a shield.

Declan rubbed his temples. "The sheriff wants you, and I need the sheriff happy, so let us just get on with it. What man in his right mind would say no to this anyway?" But Declan wanted to say no. Besides the morality of it, there was his own shame, the thing he'd kept buried and that Miss Bailey had already guessed —his inexperience. He'd kissed one woman, a childhood friend when they were adolescents, but that was the extent of his intimacies.

"You're the professional." Declan stepped next to Scarlett, who watched him curiously. "How shall we move forward?"

"Very well." Scarlett motioned for Miss Bailey to step in front of him. "Let's begin with undressing."

Declan reached for Miss Bailey's chemise, but Scarlett gently nudged his hand away. "This is her lesson, not yours."

He clenched his jaw, forcing himself to stand still as Miss Bailey stepped in front of him, her movements tentative but determined.

"Let's begin with his shirt," Scarlett instructed.

Miss Bailey's fingers found the top button, and Declan's breath caught as she dipped her index finger inside his collar, dragging it down the exposed skin of his chest. His body betrayed him, a shiver running down his spine, his cock twitching to life despite his best efforts to stay in control.

Miss Bailey glanced at him, questioning, but he kept his face impassive, giving nothing away. She gave a small shake of her head, as if to focus herself, then continued her work. Her fingers moved with more confidence as she flicked open button after button, each touch sending a pulse of heat through him. His shirt fell open, exposing his bare chest.

"Very good, Kyra," Scarlett said. "Now his trousers."

Her nails traced along his waistband, the sensation sending a jolt straight to his groin. Declan gritted his teeth, his stomach contracting pleasurably, and he held back a moan.

"Have the girls been giving you any tips?" Scarlett asked, her tone light.

Miss Bailey raised her chin proudly. "Mei and Jewell talked me through a few techniques. We practiced on a cucumber."

A startled laugh burst out of Declan before he could stop himself.

"I like your tenacity, Kyra," Scarlett said. "Just remember every man is different. You'll have to adapt."

Miss Bailey stepped behind Declan, sliding his shirt down his arms and letting it pool on the floor. Guided by Scarlett, Miss Bailey's body pressed against his back, soft against his hard muscles, and her hands slid down his abdomen.

Lust surged through him, hot and sudden, and blood rushed to his manhood, making it painfully hard. He ground his teeth, desperate to keep his face neutral, unwilling to let them see the pleasure rippling through him.

Scarlett whispered something he could not hear, and then, without warning, Miss Bailey shoved his trousers and drawers down in one swift motion, leaving him exposed.

"Oh my," Scarlett said, her eyes saucers as she stared at his saluting cock.

"What's the matter?" Declan asked, trying to keep the panic from his voice.

"You've got an impressive member, sir." Scarlett winked, and Miss Bailey's eyes darted to his cock, a flicker of worry crossing her face.

"How will I manage?" she asked, her voice a whisper. "The cucumber was not as, um, cumbersome."

Declan's cheeks burned red as the women stared at him like he was a curiosity in a circus act.

"We'll manage," Scarlett chuckled. "You're not the largest I've seen, but you're not far off. Kyra, dear, just remember what I said. When you take him into your mouth, keep your lips over your teeth. We want him to be cradled inside a soft cave, not among pointed rocks. Understand?"

Miss Bailey's face flushed, but she nodded, sinking to her knees before him, then popped her mouth open.

"Wait," Declan blurted, rocking his tip back from her lips. He feared he'd explode the moment Miss Bailey sucked him, and it would be a sure giveaway that he was as she'd accused. A virgin.

"Would you like some whiskey?" Scarlett pulled a small flask from the pocket of her dress.

Declan took it gratefully and gulped it down, hoping the burn would dull the intensity of his arousal.

"Are you relaxed now, sir?" Scarlett asked.

Declan certainly was not, standing there, naked as a babe. It seemed unfair, but he didn't dare ask Miss Bailey to undress. It would show weakness in this insane situation.

"Let's begin. Start by wetting your fingers, Kyra," Scarlett instructed.

Miss Bailey looked up at him from where she sat on her knees, wetting her fingers with deliberate slowness. Declan glowered at her, but it didn't deter her. She took her wet fingers and circled the base of his cock.

Declan clamped down on a moan, his hips bucking involuntarily at Miss Bailey's touch, electricity shooting through every nerve ending.

"Very good." Scarlett bent down and, god, it was too much having both women hover before his member. "Now wet your entire hand and stroke him. Gently. Let's see how hard you need it for maximum pleasure, Mr. Kent."

Miss Bailey did as instructed, licking her hand and wrapping it around him. Declan's head fell back, his breath coming in ragged gasps. Swirling pleasure circled his groin. He teetered on the edge of a cliff, one touch away from falling over. But he mustn't. He must hold on.

"Is that good?" Scarlett glanced up at him. He nodded once, his words stuck in his throat, unable to speak over the lust.

"Focus on the tip," Scarlett instructed. "It's the most sensitive part. But don't forget his sacs—they hold pleasure too." Scarlett bent down, her hand hovering near his balls. "May I?"

"Yes," he rasped, and she took hold of him. Declan's body jolted, his hand slamming into the dresser for support as he nearly crumbled to the floor.

"Is that good?" Scarlett asked, glancing up at him.

He managed a nod, words failing him. It was too much. Two women upon him at once, milking his cock and massaging his sacs.

Scarlett motioned to Miss Bailey. "You try."

Miss Bailey replaced Scarlett's hands with her own, her touch more tentative but no less effective. Declan's breath caught in his throat as she gently cupped his balls, her fingers rolling them in her palm. "Fascinating. They seem to have shrunk."

"It happens when the man is getting close to release," Scarlett explained with a knowing smile. "Are you close, sir?"

"Not quite," Declan hissed, but it was a lie. Every tendon in his body was tightly wound as he resisted his orgasm.

"Take him in your mouth," Scarlett instructed.

Miss Bailey dropped her hands to her lap and stared at Scarlett, hesitant. "You don't have to take it all in," Scarlett said, amused. "Use one hand at his base, like this." Scarlett wrapped her hand around him, and he sucked in a sharp breath. "Then work that hand in tandem with your mouth. Don't be afraid to use your tongue, licking his shaft as you suck."

Miss Bailey opened her mouth and bent forward, swallowing him into her cavern.

Declan cried out, gripping the dresser, his nails digging into the wood as her tongue circled his tip, sending him closer and closer to the edge.

"Jesus Christ!" The feel of her warm mouth put him into a tailspin, his body betraying him completely.

Miss Bailey pulled back, alarmed. "Did I hurt you?"

Declan squeezed his eyes shut, trying to gain control. "No," he managed. "Quite the opposite."

Miss Bailey glanced at Scarlett, unsure, but Declan nodded at her, silently entreating her to put his throbbing cock out of its misery. Finally, she leaned forward and wrapped her lips around him again. His breath hissed between his teeth, his brain spinning out, trying to think of anything to slow the oncoming storm. Her big gray eyes glanced up at him as she rocked back and forth, her mouth full of him.

That's when he lost it.

His orgasm ripped through him like a steam train. His body shuddered with the force of his release, every muscle tightening as wave after wave of pleasure surged through him. He clamped his jaw shut, desperate to keep from crying out, refusing to let her see how completely undone he was.

But it was impossible to hide the quaking of his hips, the way his legs nearly buckled beneath him as his orgasm tore through him like a wildfire. His knuckles were white, gripping the edge of the dresser for dear life, his breath coming in ragged gasps.

Miss Bailey, still on her knees, released him slowly and wiped a drop of him from the corner of her mouth. His cock nearly filled again with the rush he got from seeing his seed on her lips. Her eyes darted up to meet his, wide and filled with curiosity—innocent yet knowing all at once.

"Easy enough," Miss Bailey said, turning to Scarlett with a small, triumphant smile. "I think I can manage that with the sheriff."

Declan scowled as a possessive fire lit in his chest, unwelcome and fierce. Did she feel nothing? While he yearned to sink to the floor and bask in the thrill of what she'd done to him, her thoughts had already turned to the sheriff.

"Are we done here?" he asked, his voice harsh as he tugged his trousers back on. His hands shook with the effort of regaining control, but he refused to let either of them see it.

Scarlett smiled, clearly satisfied with how things had played out. "I'd say that was a satisfactory lesson, wouldn't you?"

Declan punched his arms into his shirt sleeves, his mind a whirl of conflicting emotions. He didn't know how to respond. He didn't know what to feel. Embarrassment? Lust? Anger? Hell, maybe all three.

As he reached for the door, he paused, turning back to Miss Bailey. "Be careful with your hands," he muttered, his voice low and rough. "You tugged too hard on my sacs."

He turned and walked out, the door slamming shut behind him. Inside his room, he fell against the wall, breathing heavily as his heart thundered in his chest. His body still thrummed with the aftershocks of what she'd done to him.

He couldn't stop images of her from playing in his mind—the way she'd looked at him, the way her lips had felt around him. *Damn her.* He wasn't supposed to want this, but she'd unlocked something in him. Something he wasn't sure he could handle.

And it had all been for the sheriff. The thought twisted his insides into knots, but what could he do? He wasn't her keeper. Not really. Hell, he didn't even know what he wanted from her, but the idea of her with another man stirred such rage in him that he wanted to tear his room apart.

Damn that woman. He would never be the same after the wicked things Miss Bailey did to him.

16

KYRA

Kyra dumped the last bucket of hot water into the tub, steam rising and filling the small, dimly lit room. The water closet, located at the end of the women's hall-way, was a luxury compared to her life in Maine. Back then, she'd lugged water from the well into the house, heating it on the kitchen stove. Here, the fireplace and pump made things easier, but no matter her efforts, the water was barely lukewarm.

Ever since her encounter with Mr. Kent earlier that night, her womanhood pulsed, yearning to be touched. Her hands tingled to give herself sweet relief, but anyone could charge in at any moment—which is exactly what happened.

"Oh, thank God. It's just you, Kyra," Mei huffed, slamming the door behind her and lifting her skirts with one hand while shoving a balled-up tea towel between her legs with the other.

"What are you doing?" Kyra asked, alarmed.

"Ice," Mei said. "I'm as chafed as a horse's back."

Before Kyra could respond, the door flew open again, and Maeve strode in with a groan. "My twat is as dry as a Texas summer."

The two women sank to the floor across from Kyra,

completely at ease in each other's presence despite the late hour. It was well after midnight, and the weight of the evening hung heavy in the air.

"How was it with Mr. Kent? I hear he's hung like an elephant's trunk." Mei smiled wickedly. Scarlett must have spoken to her.

"He was certainly larger than my husband," Kyra said, unsure how to speak of such things but finding it easier every day.

She'd been in a state after Mr. Kent left, frustrated and confused. Her first lesson with a man had been a success, but Mr. Kent had appeared almost angry, scowling as she'd sucked the marrow out of his manhood. And then, to top it off, he'd insulted her.

Still, Kyra's body was a furnace that refused to cool, left wanting after her session with Mr. Kent. Hence, her lying in a tub of lukewarm water instead of asleep in her bed. Perhaps she'd demand the sheriff help her release this fire.

"My jaw is sore," Kyra said. She hadn't meant to be droll, but Mei and Maeve bent over laughing.

"He must be really big." Mei pressed the salve harder between her legs. "I hope he never wants to bed me. I don't think little Mei Mei could handle him."

The small muscles of Kyra's sex contracted, thinking of Mr. Kent—his muscled body, his broad chest, and that massive manhood.

"Oh my God," Maeve said, her eyes alight. "You want his sausage!"

"No, I don't!" Kyra shot back, but the image Maeve painted flared in her mind before she could stop it. The way her body had responded to him was hard to ignore.

"Ain't no shame in it," Maeve said. "I miss *wanting* a man inside me. This work jades you."

They were quiet for a while. Mei and Maeve rested their heads against the wall, exhausted, and Kyra wondered if she could do this. Could she entertain multiple men night after night?

"Do you ever wish this wasn't your life?" Kyra asked. She wrapped a towel around her body and sat on the warm floor across from them.

"There are worse things than a worn-out twat," Maeve said. "Especially for a woman. We've got it better than most."

BANGING on the door startled Kyra awake. Sunlight streamed across her bed, bright and hot. It must be nearly midday. She groaned and turned over, pulling the pillow over her face.

"Miss Bailey! Get your rump out of bed," Mr. Kent's voice bellowed through the door, booming and sharp. Kyra rolled over and tried to go back to sleep.

The door flung open with a bang.

"Damn it, woman. Put some clothes on and meet me in the office," Mr. Kent barked, his voice full of irritation.

Kyra rubbed her eyes and sat up. He stood there looking altogether too composed for a man who had stormed into her room. The towel she'd fallen asleep in was bunched up beside her on the bed. Mr. Kent's eyes lingered on her bare bottom before he spun around and stomped out of the room.

Kyra groaned again, forcing herself out of bed. She grabbed a light blue cotton dress and quickly pinned up her hair, trying to ignore the flutter of nerves in her stomach. Kyra went to the kitchen, poured hot water over mint leaves, and sipped. She splashed water on her face and then knocked on the door to the office behind the bar.

"Mr. Kent?" she asked, wondering if this was regarding their activities from the previous night.

"Come in," his voice rumbled from the other side. She pushed the door open to find him seated behind the small, cramped desk, spectacles pushed up on his nose. The sight of him, somehow even more handsome with those damn glasses, was unnerving. How was it possible he could look so decent after what they'd done the night before?

"Sit," he said, barely looking up as he shuffled some papers. So he was ignoring the elephant in the room. The thought made Kyra smile, remembering Mei's comment.

"I need you to take down a letter to my mother and sister, then go to the post office and send it," he instructed.

Kyra sat, folding her hands in her lap, waiting. From his desk, Mr. Kent pulled pen and paper and held it out. Taking it from him, Kyra's fingers grazed his, and his arm shot back as if he'd had a shock.

"Dearest Mother," he began, and Kyra leaned over the desk, writing. "The situation with Clive is worse than anticipated. I must sell the saloon to secure the funds for his release. I visited him, and he is in good spirits. Once a trial date has been set, I shall send word. Give Isabella my love and tell her I will hopefully have good news for her soon. Your dearest son, Declan."

Kyra slid the letter across the desk to Mr. Kent. He picked it up, scanned the contents, and folded it into an envelope.

"Is your sister well, Mr. Kent?" she asked. She couldn't recall him ever mentioning family, save for his brother.

"Her health is strong," he replied, his tone cryptic.

Kyra hesitated, then said, "I envy you."

Mr. Kent's head snapped up, his light eyes narrowing in question.

"I envy the love you clearly share with your family. I've never known love like that." The confession surprised her, but perhaps it was the lingering intimacy of their previous encounter or the rare glimpse of humanity she saw beneath Mr. Kent's usual stern mask that made her speak this truth. Despite his gruffness, she couldn't help but admire the man who'd risked everything—leaving his life in Kentucky to save his brother, determined to make a better life for his family. His loyalty was undeniable.

"What about your husband? Your parents?" he asked.

Her response lodged in her throat, thick with sadness. Horrified at the tears threatening to spill, she looked away, shaking her head silently.

The room filled with uneasy silence. Kyra feared that if she looked at him, she'd see disgust in his eyes at her vulnerability. Besides Henry and her muddled attempt with Jacob, she'd never touched another man. The encounter with the sheriff, in her mind, was something else entirely. But what she'd done with Mr. Kent... that had been different, stirring emotions that were new and unsettling.

Finally, she glanced up, and her breath caught. His eyes held an intensity—was it concern? Affection? Whatever it was, it shook her more than his anger ever had.

"Forgive me," she murmured, her voice barely above a whisper. "I'm feeling melancholy."

"Was your husband unkind?" The force of his question sent a shiver down her spine.

"He was indifferent," she replied, bitterness coloring her tone. "Which is its own kind of cruelty. So indifferent that he left."

"Miss Bailey, I—"

She held up a hand, cutting him off and waving his concern away. She needed to change the subject before her resolve crumbled entirely. "Tell me more about your sister. Is she married?"

His gaze lingered on her for a moment longer, the softness in his expression making her pulse race. Then, as though a curtain had fallen, his face shuttered, his mask firmly back in place.

"Yes," he said, returning his attention to the papers before him. "But her husband is not kind."

"Does he—"

"Enough questions, Miss Bailey." Mr. Kent tapped the sealed envelope on the desk and handed it to her. "Mail this. Now."

Kyra stuffed the envelope in her skirt pocket, but irritated by his sudden shift back to being gruff and unreachable, she leaned in and playfully asked, "Don't you think you should call me Kyra after last night?"

In one swift motion, he reached across the desk, his hand gripping her elbow. "We will never speak of that again. Do you understand?"

If she hadn't regretted her honesty before, she certainly did now. Her vulnerability only seemed to anger him further. And yet, it also excited her. The fire that had stirred in her after their encounter ignited with the intensity of his glare.

Lifting her chin, she said with a coy smile, "I meant no offense, *sir.*"

Mr. Kent's grip tightened for a fraction of a second before he released her, sitting back in his chair. "Go to the post office. When you return, we'll discuss the inquiries about the sale."

Kyra gave a quick nod and turned to leave, but her mind spun with confusion. What in God's name was wrong with her? Somehow his fierceness made her—what did Maeve call it—*twat* pulse with a red-hot desire, yearning to finish what Mr. Kent and she had started in her room the night before.

THE ERRAND to the post office did nothing to douse the fire between her thighs or the unexpected stirrings in her chest. By the time she returned to the hotel, her frustration and need had reached a boiling point. Mr. Kent was infuriating—his moods like storm clouds ready to burst. One moment he was cold and distant, the next his gaze was warm and compassionate.

She shoved the office door open, but Mr. Kent wasn't there.

Kyra sank into the chair behind the desk and glared at the papers scattered atop it. The sweet, earthy scent of Mr. Kent lingered in the air, and it set her ablaze. Her hands clutched the arms of the wooden chair, resisting the urge to reach up her skirts. Mei had said the best way to extinguish the fire was to do it herself.

Kyra squeezed her thighs together, her drawers rubbing against her clitoris, and she moaned. She glanced around the room, her heart pounding. No one would know. She could have this small moment of relief. Her body burned with a fever that wouldn't subside. It wouldn't take long. She was sure of it.

To ensure privacy, she shoved the other chair against the door handle, then gathered her skirts above her waist and sat on the edge of the desk, spreading her legs. Her fingers moved between the slit of her drawers. Her sex was dripping, a sign that her body was readying for sexual pleasure, according to Scarlett.

Kyra circled her clit, her breath catching as her fingers found that sweet spot that was aching for release. She gasped at the shock of pleasure. Her eyes fell shut, and her hand moved faster, the heat between her legs building like wildfire.

Unbidden, images of Mr. Kent entered her mind. Naked, he'd been like a Greek statue, his muscles chiseled and taut. She'd wanted to run her hands over every ridge and valley. She imagined him standing over her, his strong hands replacing hers, his rough voice telling her what to do. The thought made her tremble.

Her fingers worked in rhythm, dipping into her wetness before circling her clit again, her hips rocking to meet each stroke. A moan escaped her lips before she could catch it, her body responding to the fantasies playing out in her mind. She imagined him naked, towering above her, his lips against her neck as he whispered things that made her pulse race.

"What in the heavens?" a voice boomed.

Kyra's eyes flew open, her body freezing in place. Mr. Kent stood in the doorway, the chair she'd used to block it knocked aside, his broad shoulders filling the frame as he stared at her with a mixture of shock and something darker, something raw.

She'd been so lost in her lustful fantasy that she hadn't heard him push into the room.

"Forgive me, Mr. Kent. I... I..." Kyra had no words. Her fiery lust turned to burning-hot humiliation.

"Were you... touching yourself?" Mr. Kent clicked the door shut, a smirk crossing his face. His gaze locked on hers before slowly dipping lower, down to where her hands had been working between her legs. The air between them thickened, heavy with tension.

Mr. Kent took another step closer, his eyes narrowing slightly as they swept over her. "I think I deserve to watch until you're finished," he said, his voice edged with humor. "An eye for an eye."

Kyra's mouth fell open. She'd expected him to storm out in anger, reprimanding her for her indecency. Not this.

"I thought we weren't talking about it?" Kyra shot back, trying to regain some semblance of control.

"You won't be talking," Mr. Kent replied, his lips curving into an amused smile. He leaned against the door, watching her like a predator cornering its prey. His commanding presence filled the room, and Kyra's heart raced in response.

Damn it all. Her body hummed with unfinished need, her mind spinning at the absurdity of the situation. She was supposed to entertain men eventually. What harm was there in starting with Mr. Kent?

With a deep breath, she lifted her skirts again, meeting his gaze with a boldness she hadn't known she possessed. If this was a game, she would play it. And she would win.

She tilted her hips toward him, opening her knees, making sure he had an ample view. When his eyes fell upon her exposed sex, all amusement left his face. His gaze locked on her body, heated and wanton. Kyra's fingers dipped between her legs once more, slick with her arousal. She swiped over her clit, letting out a soft moan as the pleasure hit her again. Her movements were slower this time, more deliberate, her gaze capturing Mr. Kent's, daring him to react.

His jaw clenched, his nostrils flaring and his gaze dropped, following the motion of her hand. His Adam's apple bobbed as he swallowed hard, and Kyra saw the telltale bulge in his trousers growing as he watched her, his breath coming in short, shallow bursts.

Her fingers moved with urgency, her hips rocking to meet the pleasure she'd denied herself her entire life. The tension between them was thick, almost suffocating, every stroke of her fingers made hotter by the knowledge that Mr. Kent watched. His restraint was palpable, his desire written in the taut line of his jaw and the fire in his gaze, even as he fought to resist his baser instincts.

The outline of his member, rock hard and ready, sent a fresh wave of heat through Kyra. She couldn't stop herself from again imagining how it would feel to have him inside her, the thought making her sex clench tightly around her fingers.

Mr. Kent's eyes followed hers to the evidence of his desire straining against his pants, then lifted back to meet her gaze. The lust etched on his face was unmistakable, and yet, he made no move to touch her. He simply watched, as she explored, stroked, and claimed her pleasure.

It was his heated stare that undid her. That unwavering hunger, that unspoken promise—*God, make it be a promise*—it was more than she could bear.

Kyra's back arched, and she cried out, her orgasm crashing over her in a tidal wave of pleasure. She couldn't stop it this time, couldn't hold back the moans as her body shook with release. She could barely breathe as the pleasure rocked through her.

She came down slowly, blinking her eyes open. Mr. Kent stood there with a ravenous hunger in his eyes, his fists clenched at his sides, and the bulge in his trousers had grown to an unmistakable size.

"Take me in your mouth," he said, his voice edged with agony.

Kyra's eyes widened, her pulse quickening at the command. "What?" she gasped, certain she'd misheard.

"Take me," Mr. Kent repeated, his eyes blazing with intensity, but there was a pleading there too. He stepped closer, towering over her as he undid his trousers with one swift motion. His thick manhood sprang free, hard and heavy, the sight of it sending another jolt of desire through her already spent body. "Like you did last night, Miss Bailey."

Kyra swallowed hard, her mouth going wet as she stared at him. He was magnificent—too magnificent, really—and the sight of him standing before her like this, so demanding, so raw, made her pulse race with a mixture of fear and excitement.

"Don't you think it's time you called me Kyra?"

17

DECLAN

If Miss Bailey—*Kyra*—didn't take care of him that instant, Declan would handle it himself, right then and there. Decency be damned.

The burn of need twisted low in his gut, each breath more strained than the last, Kyra's eyes gleaming with wicked satisfaction. But then, thank the heavens, she sank to her knees.

"I thought you said I was too rough," she teased, her breath hot against the tip of his cock, which dripped with the evidence of his desperation.

"I lied," he rasped through gritted teeth. His hands flexed above his shaft, the urge to shove her face onto his thrumming cock nearly overwhelming. But he held back. Barely.

Kyra smiled the self-satisfying grin that always made his blood boil, then parted her lips and swallowed him to the hilt.

"Christ!" The word tore from his throat as his knees buckled, his hands instinctively tangling in her hair. She worked him harder, faster than before, and all pretense of control vanished. He shoved his hands farther in her hair and pushed her closer. She coughed and sputtered, letting go of him, leaving his cock pulsing with need, desperate to expunge his seed.

"Don't do that," she hissed, her eyes flashing with irritation.

Declan held up his hands in surrender. Anything to get her mouth back on him.

With a huff, she wrapped her hand around him, her grip tight and unforgiving as she stroked him. Declan's head tipped back, a guttural moan escaping as she slid him back into her mouth, this time in full control.

"Right there," he growled, his hips rolling with each stroke. "Grab my sacs. Squeeze them."

She obliged, her hand cupping and tugging, her mouth and hand working his length with ruthless precision.

"You feel so good. It's so good..." More words tumbled out of his mouth, incoherent.

His mind went blank, his entire world narrowed to the heat of her mouth, the sensation building deep in his core until— "Oh God, yes!" His release tore through him, his body convulsing in waves so powerful he nearly collapsed on top of her, his orgasm ripping him in two.

Kyra didn't flinch, her mouth pulling every last drop from him. When she finally released him, he staggered back. His pulse pounded in his ears, and his vision blurred as he fought to regain control.

Kyra stood up, wiping her lips with the edge of her skirt as if this were nothing more than routine.

"I sent your letter, sir," she said, her tone all business now. "Is there any more servicing you need today?"

Declan cleared his throat, still breathless, fumbling to tuck himself into his trousers. "No," he spoke, the word barely audible.

"Then I shall go." Kyra scooted around him and gave a little curtsy, the picture of mock propriety, and turned to leave. But before she slipped out, she threw a glance over her shoulder, her eyes glinting with mischief. "That was your last freebie. The next time you'll have to pay, sir."

Declan opened his mouth to respond, but the door clicked shut and she was gone.

The lust-fueled high drained from his veins, leaving him cold and hollow. He sank into his chair, the weight of his choices pressing down on him like an anvil.

Kyra's absence was palpable, as if the room itself had grown heavier without her. Her earlier confession about her marriage had caught him off guard, softening something in him he'd thought impervious. *Damn it*, he'd nearly circled the desk to take her in his arms, the urge to comfort her a physical ache.

But as quickly as she'd bared that fragile part of her soul, she'd withdrawn, shutting him out.

His gaze landed on the letter from his brother's solicitor, sitting on the desk like a quiet tormentor. The request for payment mocked him, its presence a reminder of everything spiraling beyond his control. With a growl, he snatched it up, crumpling the edges before hurling it across the room.

Clive was rotting in jail. Isabella was shackled in a miserable marriage. His mother, God bless her, was alone in Kentucky, waiting for him to return. And here he was, tangled in a sordid game with a woman who should have been inconsequential—a fleeting figure in his journey. Yet, for reasons he couldn't explain, she wasn't.

He scrubbed a hand down his jaw, exhaling sharply. He needed to regain control—of himself, of this damn situation— before it all slipped through his fingers.

He adjusted his glasses, pushing them up the bridge of his nose as he reached for the day's mail. The first two letters were pathetic offers for the hotel, not even close to what the Blue-bonnet was worth. But the third... Declan's heart thundered as he read the letter from an investor keen on buying hotels across the South. Maybe, just maybe, there was a way out of this mess.

Declan nearly called Kyra back, his hand twitching toward the bell to summon her. But he stopped, his chest tightening with a pull that both frightened and infuriated him. It wasn't just desire —though that was undeniable. No, this hit deeper, sharper.

The thought of her lingered, a thorn lodged under his skin. If he indulged in what he wanted—what his entire body demanded —it wouldn't just be unwise. It would be ruinous. She wasn't a harmless distraction; she was a storm waiting to uproot everything he'd fought to build.

It nearly hurt to force the feelings down, to shove them into the deepest recesses of his mind. But he did it anyway, locking the door to those thoughts and throwing away the key. From this moment forward, he resolved to keep his distance, no matter how the sight of her—her defiance, her vulnerability, her maddening allure—stayed with him.

She was trouble. Seductive, distracting, utterly maddening trouble. And he couldn't afford it.

With deliberate care, he penned his response to the investor, then another to his brother's new solicitor. His hands shook as he wrote the final letter, the one to his banker requesting the release of his savings. The trial would be set any day now, and Declan needed funds in hand to pay the lawyer. Once that money was gone, he'd have nothing left—no savings, until the sale.

After this was all done, no matter the outcome of his brother's trial, he must return to Kentucky with haste, hat in hand, hopeful his boss would take him back.

A knock at the door startled him from his thoughts.

"A telegram has come for you, sir." Bryan placed the small piece of paper on the desk and left.

Declan's skin prickled as he unfolded the telegram, his world shifting sideways as he read.

"Bryan!" he barked, his voice sharp. Why couldn't he get a break?

The young man reappeared, wide-eyed and alarmed. "Sir?"

"Get Scarlett. Now."

Moments later, Scarlett sauntered in, her eyes flicking curiously to the telegram in Declan's hand. "You beckoned, sir?"

"What do you know of this?" Declan held the telegram out to her and watched her face closely as she read the contents, but her expression did not change.

"I'd advise you to throw that away and mind your own business," Scarlett said smoothly, slapping the telegram down in front of him.

"Is it true?"

Scarlett shrugged. "A woman doesn't become a prostitute on a whim. It's a means of survival. Think about that before you do anything that could permanently harm her."

"You'd say anything to protect Miss Bailey." Declan leaned back in his chair, steepling his fingers. The contents of the letter didn't just anger him, they twisted like a knife in his chest.

"Perhaps, but that doesn't mean what I say isn't true. My niece came to me desperate, like every other woman here. Her hell just happens to look different than the others' misfortunes."

Declan furrowed his brow, her words gnawing at the edges of his conscience. But the hell Kyra had spoken about earlier, that Scarlett hinted at now, contradicted the letter in his hand, and he didn't know what to believe.

Regardless, that telegram meant trouble.

"I can't have anything disrupting the sale of this place, and a scandal would surely do that." Declan picked the note up.

"What will you do?" Scarlett asked.

"I don't know yet. But you will respect any decision I make. Despite what you think, I want to keep this hotel intact for you and the employees here, including the women. But that might mean cutting loose the weaker links. Do you understand?"

Scarlett smiled sharply. "I understand that you'll do what's best for you."

Declan stood and rested his hands on the desk, leaning

forward. "I'll do what's best for my family like you'd do what's best for yours. We're not so different, Scarlett."

Scarlett mirrored his hands on the desk and leaned close. "Before you do anything rash, speak to her. Let her tell you her side of the story."

"Very well." Declan exhaled, the tension thick in the air. "I won't say anything yet, but I can't ignore this. I shall discover the truth," Declan said and dismissed her.

Once Scarlett left, Declan held the telegram up again, rereading it carefully:

> To the proprietor of the Bluebonnet Hotel. I am in search of my wife, Mrs. Kyra Anne Hadley. She went missing three weeks ago. Her aunt, Miss Sarah Bailey, works at the hotel and may have information. I am desperately worried. Please send a reply promptly. If I do not receive a response, I shall prepare to journey there myself and seek out my wife's aunt for information. I am desperate to find my dear wife.
>
> Awaiting your reply, I remain, yours truly,
> Mr. Henry Hadley, Professor of Mathematics,
> Bates College, Lewiston, Maine

Declan shoved the telegram in a side drawer and slammed it shut, resisting his urge to charge into Kyra's room and demand an explanation, to beg her to tell him it was a lie.

Obviously, Sarah Bailey was Scarlett's given name, which Kyra must have adopted when she arrived.

He needed more information before he did anything rash. If Kyra left her husband instead of the other way around, she could have a good reason for running off, and he didn't want to put her in harm's way.

No matter the truth, there would be trouble if her husband journeyed to Wylde as he threatened in the correspondence. In a rush, Declan penned a letter. He needed to know more about this Henry Hadley before he spoke to Kyra, and if his claims were true. But one thing was certain. Kyra had lied about more than just her name.

18

KYRA

Kyra lay sprawled on her bed staring at the stained ceiling, a small smile on her face. The past few weeks had transformed her from a respectable young lady to a woman who had sexually pleasured two men—and herself— with almost no shame.

A week had passed since she'd been with Declan in his office, yet the memory of him, a man so buttoned up and in control coming apart in her hands, made her pulse quicken every time it crossed her mind. She could still feel the warmth of his skin, the tension in his body as he lost himself to her touch.

There was no going back now—not to Henry, not to her old life. The moment she'd taken the sheriff into her room and demanded he stroke his manhood, her fate was sealed.

She craved this new path. As strange and confusing as all this was, it was also exhilarating. For the first time, she was doing what she wanted. Every encounter left her feeling bolder, more alive. One day she'd be jaded like Mei and the other girls, but for now, she felt something else entirely: liberation.

But one thing kept nagging at the back of her mind. She'd continued her lessons with Scarlett without resistance, but

Declan had been distant. Tension rolled off him in waves, an angry fire simmering just under the surface, a fire that felt directed at her. It upset her more deeply than she wanted to admit.

Kyra hadn't been with another man since that day with Declan, but she'd witnessed more acts, understood what would be required of her once she began working in earnest. Each new experience awakened something within her—her blood dancing through her veins with newfound possibility.

Was Declan angry because her sexual awakening gave her a sense of control, while he seemed to lose more of his with every encounter? Or was it because she was withholding sex from him without payment? It had been a whimsical move. Not that he'd asked to be with her since that day.

Instead of relief, sorrow pulled at her chest. She'd been moved by the letter to his mother. He loved his family, and his goal was to care for them. It had unexpectedly raised sympathy in her for his situation, and she wasn't exactly thrilled by it. She didn't want anything standing between her and the new life she was creating.

Kyra flipped to her belly and groaned into her pillow. She was meant to see the sheriff that night, but with all these racing thoughts, she was in no mood to do anything. Back in Maine when she was overwhelmed, she'd slip into her swim costume and go to the river. And suddenly, that was exactly what she needed.

Kyra got up and knocked on the doors of the other girls, rounding them up. "We need an adventure," she announced when they gathered, groaning in their half-dressed states.

"What kind of adventure?" Maeve asked, yawning.

"There's a creek about a mile out of town. We're going swimming. We can borrow a wagon from the hotel, or walk."

"Swimming?" Jewell raised a brow.

"It'll be refreshing," Kyra insisted.

The girls grumbled but eventually relented, pulling on their clothes and following her out to the stables. After hitching up a wagon, they piled in and Kyra took the reins. The sun blazed overhead as they made their way out of town, the dusty road stretching ahead of them.

"I can't swim," Jewell confessed from the back of the wagon.

"Or me," said Mei from her perch beside Kyra.

"We'll find a shallow spot," Kyra said, guiding the horses off the main road to a shaded path. Kyra was good at finding water, especially in a place as dry as Texas. Trees and vegetation thrived and thickened near water. She'd spent years seeking out creeks and rivers to escape to, and sure enough, they soon came upon a slow-moving creek with a long rock bed.

The women stripped down to their undergarments and slid into the cool water. It was only a few inches deep where they entered, with a lazy current. Kyra scooted farther into the deeper section, luxuriating in the cool water rushing over her back and shoulders.

It was a brief reprieve from the chaos of her life. For a few moments, she could pretend she was back in Maine, floating in the Androscoggin River, where she'd escape to be free from Henry's sour moods and constant belittling.

"Why did your husband leave?" Jewell asked from her perch on a log that jutted out over the water.

"Jewell!" Mei scolded, splashing her.

"It's alright," Kyra said, swimming back toward them. For a moment, Kyra considered telling them the truth: Henry hadn't left. She'd run out on him.

She'd told no one, not even her aunt, fearing it would get back to Declan. Secrets had a way of coming out. Instead, she told another truth.

"I can't have children," she stated quietly, the familiar grief unfurling in her chest.

"In our line of work, that's a blessing," Jewell said, tipping her face up to the sun.

Jewell was right. Kyra knew that. It was the reason she had finally gathered the courage to leave Henry. But it didn't make the pain any less real.

"I wasn't always barren," Kyra confessed. "Henry and I had a shotgun wedding when I was seventeen. He'd courted me, the portrait of a gentleman, and after six months, we consummated the relationship. In my naivety, I assumed it meant we were engaged, but he refused me. He said he was in love with another woman."

"What a bastard," Maeve muttered in her Irish brogue, shaking her head.

"You can guess what happened next," Kyra continued. "I was late for my monthly, and my belly grew like a watermelon. Henry had no choice but to marry me."

Their wedding night was the first time he drank himself into a stupor.

"A month later, I lost the baby," Kyra said, her chin wobbling. She ground her jaw until the jagged pain turned to a dull ache and she could speak again. "And then I lost the next one. And the next. After that, it had happened too many times to count."

"Did you tell him to keep his snake away from you?" Mei asked, her eyes wide.

Kyra laughed at Mei's bluntness, feeling a tad lighter. "I did, actually. I think he was relieved, but then he came home one night drunk." She hesitated, the memory still raw. "He didn't force me. But I did what I was taught to do as a good wife."

"And you got pregnant again," Jewell finished softly.

Kyra nodded, her throat tightening. "But something went wrong. I lost the baby, and that time, it damaged me permanently."

The water rippled around her as silence fell over the group.

"You left him, didn't you?" Maeve said, as if it all made sense now. "He didn't leave you."

Kyra nodded, unable to lie. She hadn't meant to reveal so

much, but the truth had come tumbling out. "Please don't say anything. If the law finds out, I'll be shipped back to Maine."

"What if he comes looking for you?" Maeve asked, brushing her fiery-red hair out of her face.

"He won't. He'll be glad I'm gone. I bet he went straight to Betty."

"Who's Betty?" Mei asked.

Maeve pushed her foot into Mei's thigh. "The woman he was in love with, obviously."

"You're right. Betty was his childhood sweetheart, but she became engaged to another man. That's why he courted me. But her husband died two years after our wedding in a boating accident. That's when Henry's drinking went from mild to extreme. He wanted to be with her, but he was stuck in a loveless marriage with me."

"That's so sad," Mei said.

Jewell rolled her eyes. "You're such a romantic."

Mei smiled, taking it as a compliment.

"It's vexing to consider," Kyra pondered. "But my biggest loss—never being able to have children—is what ultimately led to my freedom."

"Well, you're here now. And you have a lot of life left. You're about twenty-five, right?" Jewell said, kicking at the water playfully. "And no one's taking you back to Maine."

Kyra forced a smile, but deep down she knew her freedom was still precarious. If Henry ever came looking for her...

"Let's not talk about that," she said, pushing the thoughts away. "We're supposed to be having fun."

THERE WAS laughter and chitchat on the ride back to town, the kind of easy camaraderie Kyra had never experienced before. The women teased and joked as they rode, their bonds growing stronger with each passing minute. For the first time in her life, she had real friends, women who understood her, who accepted her. It filled her with a warmth she hadn't experienced in years.

But her good mood vanished the moment they returned to the hotel.

Declan Kent stood on the raised sidewalk in front of the building, his face a thundercloud of fury, a piece of paper gripped in one of his fists.

"Where have you been?" He pointed an accusing finger at Kyra.

Kyra's heart skipped. "I—"

"In my office. Now."

She debated ignoring him, but she knew better. Delaying him would only make things worse.

"Go on," Jewell whispered with a wink. "I'm sure he's just mad you didn't invite him swimming."

Kyra shot her a glare before turning and following Declan into his office, her heart pounding in her chest. She had a feeling that whatever waited for her behind that door would change everything.

19

DECLAN

"You're a liar." Declan leaned against the edge of his desk, arms crossed, glaring at Kyra behind his glasses.

She didn't flinch, meeting his gaze with equal fire. "I am no liar, sir."

Declan's mind flicked back to the very spot where he leaned now—the same spot where he'd found her a week ago, skirts hiked up, fingers teasing herself. The memory flooded his mind, heat surging through him like wildfire before he tamped it down.

He'd been a fool to get caught up in her seductions. Was it all a game to her? Some twisted play where he was the toy and she the puppet master?

In the letter Declan had written to Bates College the week before, he'd posed as a former student, inquiring whether a Professor Hadley still taught there. If he was still there, then he couldn't have run out on Kyra. Next, he'd telegrammed the county clerk's office in Lewiston, requesting a record of Henry and Kyra's marriage license. The county had been swift in their reply, sending a copy of the license. Henry Hadley was indeed Kyra's husband.

But Declan had held off confronting Kyra until he received a response from Bates College, and the letter had arrived that morning. The college confirmed what he had suspected all along: Henry Hadley was teaching that semester. Which meant Kyra's husband hadn't left her—she'd left him.

The letter also noted that Professor Hadley would only be on campus for another week before their summer break began, which meant by now the term had ended, and Kyra's husband could arrive any day if he followed through on the promise he'd made in the original telegram.

All week Declan had steered clear of Kyra, but there was no holding back now. Everything Declan had feared was true. If Henry showed up, he could sue the Bluebonnet or Declan, invoking morality or vagrancy laws. Or worse, he could uncover the truth about Kyra's work at the Bluebonnet.

Either scandal could ruin everything and put Declan and his family in danger.

"Explain to me again why you're here," he said, his anger barely held in check, waiting for more lies.

"You asked me to come."

"Don't be clever with me," he snapped. "Why are you here, at the Bluebonnet, training to be a whore?"

Kyra's gaze flicked to his trousers, one brow arching. "I think my training is complete, don't you, sir?"

Declan shifted, willing his traitorous body to behave. "That was an unfortunate lapse in judgment," he ground out. "One that won't happen again. Now answer the question."

Kyra sighed dramatically. "My husband left me. I needed a way to make a living. I can't remarry because he hasn't divorced me, so here I am. Coming to my aunt was the only practical option."

Declan shook his head, his disbelief mounting. Still lying. He circled the desk, his movements slow and deliberate as he pulled open a drawer. He took out the telegram from her husband and the marriage license and placed them on the desk in front of him, watching her eyes flick to the pieces of paper, her curiosity piqued.

"And why did your husband run off?" He sat in his chair and leaned back, his gaze never leaving her face.

Kyra's hand instinctively moved to her belly, a nervous gesture he'd noticed before. "I can't have children. My womb rejects them. He wants a family, and I... I can't give him one." She sounded defiant, but her voice caught at the end, betraying the pain behind the words.

Declan's heart clenched. Despite her lies, he suspected this part of the story was true.

"If he wants a family so badly, why didn't he divorce you and find another wife?" Declan asked, his anger ebbing.

Kyra blinked, her cheeks cresting pink. "I... I don't know. The scandal of divorce, I suppose."

"Your story doesn't line up, Miss Bailey. Care to try again?" He adjusted his glasses as she squirmed.

"That is the truth, sir." Kyra jutted her chin.

"Is it, Mrs. Hadley?"

"Yes! I—" Kyra gasped. "What did you call me?"

"Mrs. Henry Hadley." Declan pushed the telegram and license across the desk.

Kyra snatched the telegram first, her eyes flying across the paper. Her face paled as she read it, her grip tightening on the note. "No," she whispered, her voice small, trembling. She glanced at the marriage license in front of her. "No..."

"You were not abandoned," Declan said, his tone icy, "and your husband is searching for you. What do you think will happen when he finds out where you've been hiding? When he discovers you've been working in a brothel? He could bring a scandal that would put me in the same jail cell as my brother."

Declan's voice rose as his anger flared. He shot out of his chair, towering over her. "Did you think about that? Did you think about the people you'd hurt?"

"I had to leave him!" Kyra shouted, stepping back, her eyes blazing with desperation. "You spoke of your sister. You said she's in a bad marriage. What would she do if she were in my shoes?"

Declan's heart pounded in his chest. He wanted to stay angry, wanted to hold on to the fury that had fueled him moments ago, but her words struck a sympathetic chord deep within him. Was she lying again, or was there truth to her plea?

"You've put everyone here at risk." He sank back into his chair, rubbing his temples. "If your husband comes looking and raises hell, this place—everything—could be destroyed. Did you really believe he wouldn't think to look for you here?"

"I wasn't thinking," Kyra cried, her gloved fists balling at her sides. "I couldn't stay there. I was trapped. We only got married because I was with child. And then I lost it. Again and again. I lost all of them."

Kyra pressed the back of her hand to her lips, holding back the torrent of emotion that threatened to spill out. Declan's chest tightened as he watched her crumble, her vulnerability laid bare in front of him.

"Henry never loved me." Kyra stared furiously at Declan, tears in her eyes. "He married me out of duty, but he resented me for it. I was alone, hiding from his drunken fits. After the last loss, he promised he wouldn't touch me again, said my womb was cursed. But it happened one more time, and that last pregnancy nearly killed me. I can never have children. I left because I was afraid he'd take what little was left of me."

Kyra's pain was palpable, a woman broken by loss, running from a life that had nearly destroyed her.

"It was shortsighted of you." He turned around and looked out the small window, his back to her. He couldn't look at her. If he did, he might do something stupid like snatch her in his arms and kiss her. "You didn't think."

The floorboards creaked as Kyra moved behind him. The air shifted, carrying her warmth across the inches between them.

Her hands slid around his waist, her hips pressing against his backside. If only she touched him with true affection, but this was a seduction, a way to manipulate him.

"Don't," he growled, spinning to face her. He shoved her away and she stumbled, hitting the wall with a soft cry. "You're married!" Declan's voice boomed in the small room, echoing off the walls. "What we've done... it's unspeakable."

"You knew I was married before," Kyra said, her voice shaking, clutching her shoulder where it had hit the wall.

"Not like this," Declan spoke roughly. He dropped his forehead into his hands, shaking it back and forth. "To think what we did. What I've allowed you to do here. My God."

Kyra stepped forward, her gaze imploring. "Henry won't come after me. He doesn't care enough to cause trouble."

"You have no idea what a humiliated man will do," Declan said. "Men have started wars for far less than this."

"Then write to him," Kyra pleaded. "Tell him I'm not here."

"I will not lie."

"Then you'll bring this place down." Desperation laced her words.

Declan's hand shot out, grabbing her arm and pulling her close, his voice a low growl. "Don't ever blame me for what you've done. Do you hear me? It was you who ran away and put these women in harm's way. Even if I wrote that lie, your husband will eventually come, and when he does, this whole place will fall—your aunt's empire, these girls, everything."

Kyra stared up at him, tears brimming in her eyes. For a moment, neither of them moved, the weight of the truth heavy between them.

"I'm sorry," she whispered. "I never meant for any of this to happen."

Declan loosened his grip on her arm, stepping back. His mind raced, torn between anger, guilt, and something far more threatening that simmered just beneath the surface.

"I don't know what to do," Kyra admitted, her voice soft, almost broken.

"Nor do I." Declan shook his head, defeated and unsure. "But your presence here if Henry arrives is a risk I cannot take. I'm sorry, Miss Bailey, but you must leave."

20

KYRA

Kyra flew out of Declan's office, her heart pounding as though it might leap from her chest. She barely made it to the hallway before the tears she'd been holding back spilled out. How could she have been so stupid? Did she really believe Henry would let her go so easily?

Yes. That was exactly what she'd believed. How many times had Henry mumbled his regrets in marrying her? But now, faced with the cold reality of Henry's telegram, Kyra realized that pride could make a man do foolish, dangerous things.

But she couldn't go back to Maine. She'd meant it when she'd told Declan that place would kill her. Not by Henry's hand; she'd wither away from heartbreak. The house was a mausoleum of all those lost souls her body had rejected.

After all the years, there'd still been a shred of hope that a baby would fill the rooms of her home with love one day. But all that hope died with the last miscarriage, and she couldn't bear to live a moment longer in the ruins of her lost dreams. The promise of a child had kept her in her marriage. Her parents were gone, she had no siblings, and Henry never loved her. A child was the one thing that could've filled the cavern that had become her heart.

Once that died, so did everything else.

Kyra's steps quickened as she reached her room. She had no time to indulge in regrets. Her hands shook as she threw her belongings into her luggage, her mind racing with options. Henry might not come, but the threat of him finding her was too much.

Henry could have her arrested for desertion, since she left without his consent. She knew these laws all too well, having spent extra time raking over them. He could argue that she was violating her legal and moral obligation to remain with him. That alone would provide grounds for her arrest.

Sheriff Mack was fond of her, but there was no reason to believe he'd bend the law to help her. Even asking him would put her freedom in danger. No, she had to do as Declan demanded. She had to leave.

There was a town in South Dakota where women could file for divorce after only three months of residency. It would be a long journey north, and she barely had enough money to make it out of Texas, let alone all the way to Sioux Falls. She'd spent most of her savings traveling here, but she'd have to find a way north. Declan had made it clear he would not harbor a would-be fugitive.

Dragging her luggage, Kyra made her way to her aunt's room, careful to avoid Declan. Scarlett was savvy. Perhaps she'd have a solution or, if nothing else, would lend Kyra money for her journey.

Kyra's small fists banged the door. Scarlett swung it open and ushered Kyra inside, eyeing her luggage. The room matched Scarlett's name, with crimson curtains and bedding, and bloodred lace covering the surfaces. Her aunt even wore a ruby silk robe with large white flowers, a style that Kyra had seen in *Harper's Bazaar*.

"Declan showed you the telegram," Scarlett said. It wasn't a question. "And now he's kicked you out."

"You knew?" Kyra sank onto the bed, her shoulders slumping.

Scarlett sighed and sat beside her. "I begged him to wait and talk to you so you could explain yourself."

"I did," Kyra whispered, shaking her head. "He says I'll bring the entire place down if I'm found here. And he's not wrong. What was I thinking coming here? I should've gone straight to South Dakota. Instead, I've used up the little savings I had, and I've made things worse."

"Sioux Falls isn't some magical haven for women seeking divorce. The locals treat them like outcasts. The only women who survive there are the ones with money and time to waste." Scarlett's gaze softened, but her words held a bite of truth.

Kyra sniffed. "But there's an enclave of women that live there, waiting for their divorce. They have their own community. I hoped to be a part of that."

"Rich women who can afford to sit around and wait for months. Not people like us."

Tears dripped down Kyra's cheeks. "I'm a fool."

"You're a woman. And women have to make impossible choices every day," Scarlett said firmly, placing a hand on her knee.

"What should I do now?" Kyra asked, feeling the walls of her life closing in.

Scarlett's lips quirked into a sly smile. "You're not going anywhere. Write a note to Mr. Kent saying you've left. Then hide here in my room until I can figure out the rest."

Kyra blinked. "But—"

"Hush," Scarlett interrupted, her eyes sparkling with a dangerous edge. "Let me handle this."

Doubt gnawed at Kyra's insides, but there was something reassuring in the way Scarlett took control of the situation. She had to trust someone, and Scarlett was her only option. Quickly,

Kyra penned the note and handed it to her aunt, watching as Scarlett swept out of the room, skirts swishing in her wake.

Time dragged as Kyra waited, her mind spinning with a thousand "what-ifs." Finally, Scarlett returned, a triumphant smile curling her lips.

"He has accepted the lie." Scarlett smiled like the cat who ate the cream. "I told him you slid the note under my door, and when I checked, all your things were gone. I made Mr. Kent promise to telegram Henry that you'd fled a week ago when you saw his message. Hopefully, it will stall Henry for now."

"Mr. Kent will be furious if he finds out we've lied," Kyra said, glancing out the window. Scarlett pulled the curtains shut so no one could look up into the second story and see Kyra.

"He won't find out. I pretended to be furious at him. I threatened to take my girls and leave. In fact, I told him we shall all keep our legs shut until he changes his mind and lets you come back."

"You didn't!" Kyra flung her feet to the ground from the bed and walked up to her aunt.

"Don't worry, child. We aren't really stopping business," Scarlett said. "I've already told Bryan to pass along a message to our regulars. We'll take clients in the rooms above the stables for the time being. It's not ideal, but it's better than nothing. We had to be discreet once before when a traveling minister came to town and put up a fuss about the brothel. That minister didn't last long."

"What will you tell the sheriff?" Kyra bit her lip, still unsure. "He'll wonder about my absence."

"Don't worry about him. I'll keep him distracted."

Kyra leaned against the dresser, exhaling a sigh. "Perhaps I should just go home and accept my fate."

"Nonsense. We just have to keep hidden until Henry's off the scent and no longer a threat to the saloon. Then we'll tell Mr. Kent the truth, that you never left. Mr. Kent's not wrong. Henry could cause some real problems for us, and it's better if he thinks you're not here."

"I understand," Kyra relented. "I'm furious at Mr. Kent, but I'm more furious with myself."

"Stop that. I'll do everything I can to keep you safe. You're my only kin."

Kyra stared at her aunt, warmth blooming in her chest. Scarlett had stood up for her, and it felt... good. She hadn't been shown kindness like that in a long time.

"Thank you," Kyra whispered, her voice thick with emotion.

Scarlett's eyes softened, but she didn't dwell on sentimentality. "Stay quiet when you're in here. Declan has keys to every room, but he rarely comes to mine. I must go now. I've got preparations to make for the night."

As Scarlett slipped into a simple dress, ready to handle whatever came next, Kyra couldn't help the flicker of hope that sparked inside her.

"What if Mr. Kent discovers me?" Kyra asked, a mix of fear and anticipation thrumming in her veins.

Scarlett glanced over her shoulder with a wicked grin. "We'll just have to make sure he doesn't, won't we?"

DECLAN

The saloon was disturbingly quiet, as if the life had been sucked from the very walls. No bawdy music, no laughter, no clinking of coins tossed toward the stage. Just the hollow murmur of a few lingering travelers nursing their drinks, disappointed that the regionally famous Bluebonnet Belles were nowhere to be seen.

Declan had thought pulling the girls was an empty threat from Scarlett. He hadn't imagined she'd follow through, and now, with the absence of her women, the saloon was losing money. Enzo had already tossed more than one rowdy customer out on the street. Travelers came expecting a show, and finding none, they weren't happy.

Declan's gaze drifted to the saloon doors, half-expecting Kyra to saunter in, flashing him that infuriating mix of defiance and allure that had always set his blood boiling. But of course, she wouldn't. She'd gone.

When Declan confronted Kyra earlier, his words had been sharp and rash. He hadn't intended to force her out. The moment the heat of the argument cooled, regret set in like a dagger to his gut.

He'd been on his way to make amends, to tell her what he hadn't been ready to admit even to himself. Her confession—the heartbreaks that had shaped her, the quiet strength that kept her standing—had shattered his defenses. He didn't want her gone. He wanted her here, in his life, as much a part of it as his own breath. Protector, not tormentor. He wanted to be the man she could lean on.

But she'd left before he could say any of it.

When Scarlett had handed him the note, a cold knot of disbelief formed in his chest. He'd rushed to Kyra's room, half-hoping the message had been some cruel joke. But her room was bare—her belongings gone, her presence erased as though she'd never been there at all.

Had she taken the train? That seemed most likely. She had no horse, and there were no coaches leaving Wylde that afternoon. And as far as Declan knew, she didn't know anyone in town except for the girls and, perhaps, the sheriff—but he doubted she'd gone to him.

The note had been clear: she wasn't coming back.

Declan stood, staring at the empty saloon, feeling the strange, hollow wrench in his chest that came with her absence.

He exhaled, rubbing the back of his neck. His mind kept returning to the sorrow in her voice, the way she spoke of her lost children, her shattered hopes. It had hit him hard, and now he was left with a gnawing guilt. His anger had forced her hand, and he'd driven her away.

He squeezed his eyes shut as if that would squeeze out the hurtful words he'd yelled at Kyra.

Unsettled, Declan walked up the stairs to the side of the hotel where the women's rooms were located. He'd expected them to be lounging and conversing—or sneaking johns upstairs behind his back. But it was quiet and empty.

Declan knocked on Scarlett's door. No answer. He tried the

handle. Locked. He knocked again, listening for any sound inside, but none came. Where the hell had they all gone?

Walking down the hallway, he threw open each door. The women's belongings, clothing, hairbrushes, and ribbons were strewn about their rooms. They were clearly still in residence, but they weren't here.

"May I help you, Mr. Kent?" It was Mei, the pretty young Chinese girl. She looked lovely in her silk robe, her dark hair falling in waves around her shoulders, ruby-red lips quirked into a half smile. "I can't provide you company tonight, but if you'd like a rain check..."

Her index finger trailed down his arm, her touch light, teasing. Declan took a step back, clearing his throat. "Where is everyone?"

"Out for a walk."

"At midnight?" Declan scoffed. "I hardly believe it."

Mei shrugged. "It's a beautiful night, and the girls are used to being up late. They needed something to do."

"Why aren't you with them?" he asked, eyeing her.

She flicked her gaze over her right shoulder, toward the back stairs that led to the small stables. "I prefer quieter company," she said, batting her lashes.

Declan wasn't buying it. "You're done up rather fancy for a night in."

"I like to look pretty with or without a man to please." Mei brushed past Declan. "Have a good evening, sir."

Declan watched her sashay down the hallway. "One moment, Mei." She paused, turning slightly. "Do you know where Miss Bailey went?"

Mei's lips curved into a smile. "Back to her husband, I presume."

"Is that what she told you?"

"No." Mei's smile didn't falter. "But what choice does she

have?" With that, she disappeared down the stairs, leaving Declan more unsettled than before.

The tremor of fear in Kyra's voice as she'd talked about her past had stayed with him, gnawing at his conscience.

Declan turned, heading back to his room, his thoughts tangled in confusion and guilt. He locked the door behind him and sank into his chair, his body aching with exhaustion. He was tired. So damn tired. All he wanted was for his brother to be free, his family safe, and to get the hell out of this place.

He groaned, rubbing his hands over his face, and tried to shake off the cloying feeling in his gut.

At one time, he had thought Kyra leaving would give him peace. But instead, he was more distraught than ever. She'd found a sliver of liberation in this brothel, and he'd taken that from her.

Declan leaned back in his chair, staring at the ceiling, making a decision. If he ever saw her again, he wouldn't abandon her. He'd protect her as he would his sister, his family.

22

KYRA

By the fifth day of isolation in Scarlett's room, Kyra was as restless as a tiger in a cage. It was early, the sun barely rising. Scarlett slept on the bed beside her, snoring like a well-fed bear.

What was she doing? Kyra couldn't stay in the room forever. Even if Henry left her alone, would Declan Kent relent and let her stay in Wylde? Doubtful. Not after he discovered she'd lied to him.

Kyra slid off the bed, the ropes groaning, but Scarlett's snoring didn't falter. She slipped on a forest-green cotton dress and pinned her fair blonde locks up. Then she snuck down the back stairs and into the alley. When she cleared the yard without anyone spying her, she let out a relieved breath. She couldn't stand being cooped up one more minute.

The early morning air was fresh, crisp even, the promise of heat still hours away. As she'd predicted, no one was on the dirt road that led to the farms on the outskirts of town. She walked huddled against the tree line, her ears open to the sounds of hoofbeats, but none came. She'd snatched an apple Scarlett had left for her and a ratty towel. Her destination, the creek.

At the bubbling stream, Kyra stripped out of her garments and slid into the cool water. She dunked her head, letting the weight of the water wash away the tension coiling inside her.

After drying off on the sun-drenched bank, she slipped back into her dress. Red dirt clung to her hem as she headed back to town, her hair a hopeless tangle.

As she neared town, hoofbeats alerted her to someone approaching. She scurried into the trees and tucked behind a large maple, her heart hammering. A moment later, the rider appeared—Declan. She gasped and tucked farther into the brush. He rode by, his expression as hard and unyielding as ever. He looked healthy and alive. Not like the solemn man who'd first arrived. His skin was golden, his frame stronger. Even Blaze, his horse, looked refreshed.

She stayed hidden until he disappeared around a bend, then she stepped out onto the road again, sure the danger had passed.

But it hadn't. Another rider, faster this time, appeared before she could duck back into the trees. The sun, blazing behind him, cast the man in silhouette, but she didn't need to see his face to know who it was.

Kyra shot her head around her, looking for an escape, but there was none.

"Kyra?" the man said in shock.

"Hello, Henry." She kept her voice steady despite her rapid heartbeat.

Her husband dismounted and rushed to Kyra, wrapping his arms around her and squeezing her to his chest. She wiggled out of his embrace and looked into his face. His chestnut hair was longer, but it suited him. His eyes were clear, and his skin glowed in a way it hadn't before. And his smell... it was crisp and spicy. Clean. Sober.

"What are you doing here?" Kyra asked, looking down the road as if it might hold the answer.

"I came for you," Henry said, his voice soft but insistent. "I arrived yesterday, went straight to your aunt's saloon, and spoke with the owner, Mr. Kent. He claimed he didn't know you. Even Scarlett denied you were there. But here you are." He stood back and waited for her explanation.

"I..." She faltered, speechless. Not because Henry was there, though that was startling, but because Declan had lied for her.

"I used my maiden name," Kyra stammered. "They wouldn't have known me as Mrs. Hadley."

"But I showed him your picture."

The only photo she'd ever taken was on her wedding day. "My likeness has changed over the years," she said, covering for Declan's lies.

"Your aunt would know you." Henry studied her, suspicious.

"She hasn't seen me since I was a young child."

Henry nodded, but Kyra wasn't sure she'd convinced him. Before he could press further, a set of hoofbeats echoed down the road. Declan rode up, reining Blaze to a halt beside them.

"Professor. There you are. I thought you were just behind me." Declan's eyes flashed with surprise when he spied her.

"Miss Bailey," he said with an edge to his voice. "What in tarnation are you doing out here? You should be stripping the sheets and tidying the guests' rooms."

Kyra's heart skipped a beat. He was keeping up the charade.

"I needed some air," she stammered, trying to play along. "Didn't sleep much."

"My apologies, Professor Hadley. This is one of my newer employees, Miss Bailey. She's a maid at the hotel."

Why was he protecting her? Was it so Henry wouldn't sue him if the truth of her activities at the brothel came out? Or was there a nobler reason?

Henry laughed like this was all some grand misunderstanding. "No need for apologies. Seems my wife has fooled us both."

Declan did a good job of appearing shocked by this information. "Good God, man. This is your wife? I had no idea."

"No matter. I've found her now and that's all that matters." Henry's arm snaked around Kyra's waist. "Seems she thought hiding out as a maid would do the trick."

"Let us go back to the hotel and discuss this matter," Declan said, rounding them with his horse. "I had no idea I was harboring a runaway wife." Declan slid off his horse and offered it to Kyra for the short journey back to the saloon.

"So you're a maid at the hotel?" Henry appeared relieved. "I thought you'd come to ask your aunt for a, um... position at the saloon. You often spoke in envy of Scarlett's business."

"I was envious of the freedoms it allowed her, but that is not the life for me," Kyra lied, mounting Blaze.

"And cleaning chamber pots and linens is?" Henry pressed, a slight edge in his voice.

"I'm sorry, my love," Kyra said. "After the last... after what happened, I went a little mad."

"Plainly." He frowned. "You look dreadful."

Kyra's cheeks burned and she glanced down at Declan, but he stared at the road ahead, not acknowledging anything she or Henry said.

"I... it's been a rough few days."

"When we're back at the hotel, clean up, and we'll discuss your return to Maine. I can't have you looking like a gypsy. I told everyone you went to visit an aunt on the coast to rest by the seaside. You can't come back looking more haggard than when you left."

"Of course, dear," Kyra said, placating him, her mind spinning. Her adventure had come to an end so abruptly, she could hardly grasp it.

Kyra wondered if she told him the truth—that she'd been training as a prostitute and had been with two different men since she arrived—would he be so disgusted that he'd allow for a divorce? Or would he use it against her somehow?

Declan cleared his throat. "It seems there's a lot to discuss when we get back to the hotel."

Kyra tried to catch Declan's gaze, but he wouldn't look at her. What had happened in the past few days to cause Declan to protect her secret?

She supposed it didn't matter. She'd be gone from there soon enough, and this would all feel like a dream.

23

DECLAN

eclan's heart had lurched in his chest when he'd spotted Kyra by the side of the road, engaged in conversation with her husband, Professor Hadley. He'd had to grip his thighs against Blaze's body to resist the urge to leap down, pull Kyra into his arms, and assure himself that she was real and not an illusion from the heat of the midday sun. The fear that he'd never see her again had haunted him since the moment she left after their fight.

When Professor Hadley had shown up at the hotel the previous day—alone and inquiring about his wife—Declan's protective instincts had kicked into high gear. He'd swiftly penned a note to Scarlett, informing her of the professor's presence and urging her to feign ignorance about Kyra's presence ever at the hotel.

Declan had pretended he had no knowledge of the "Mrs. Hadley" the professor was seeking.

As they rode back to the hotel, the sunlight caught Kyra's golden hair just so, making his heart flutter. Declan's hand twitched on Blaze's neck, desperate to get closer—to pull her away from that man.

Kyra's gaze bore into Declan, but he avoided her eyes. He wasn't ready to face the questions she must have, the explanations he owed her.

Upon their arrival at the hotel, Kyra hastened to the washroom to freshen up, while Declan beckoned Mei.

"Please move Professor Hadley's belongings into Miss Bailey's room," he instructed, despite the sharp pain that hit him in his chest. The thought of them together under the same roof—let alone in the same bed—burned like a hot brand on his heart.

To his surprise, Professor Hadley waved off the suggestion. "That won't be necessary," he said, his tone dismissive. "I'll keep my separate room."

Declan's brow furrowed. For a man who had traveled across the country to find his wife, the professor seemed oddly disinterested in spending time with her. Instead, he made a beeline for the bar, ordering a whiskey and settling onto the barstool. The professor was of average height, with neatly trimmed hair slicked back with pomade. He was lean and sat rigidly on the stool as he gulped his drink, quickly asking for another.

Dismissing the unease in his gut, Declan retreated to his office and tried to focus on the never-ending paperwork that came with running the Bluebonnet. But his mind kept wandering back to Kyra, returned to the hotel, and the puzzle that was her husband.

Professor Hadley had been controlled and hadn't touched a drop of liquor since his arrival, until now. Something about being in Kyra's presence agitated him. It was odd that the professor didn't want to be in the same hotel room as his wife. If it were Declan, he'd be with Kyra now, locking the door and not coming out again until morning, enjoying her company thoroughly. Why come for Kyra if Professor Hadley didn't truly want her?

An hour later, Declan was staring at the same row of numbers when a commotion from the bar jolted him from his chair. He rushed out to investigate and found a scene of utter chaos.

Professor Hadley, sloppy from the libations, dragged Kyra from table to table, his grip on her arm rough and unyielding. Jewell, Mei, and Maeve watched in shocked silence, while the patrons looked on with delight, excited for something more than the usual bar brawl.

"How many of you have slept with my wife?" Professor Hadley slurred, his voice rising. "That's why she's here, isn't it? To lie down for any man who'll have her, to humiliate me!"

Kyra's face reflected her mortification, her eyes glistening with unshed tears. Declan's blood boiled at the sight.

"Let her go, Hadley," he growled, striding forward and placing himself between the professor and Kyra. "No man here has slept with your wife."

Declan respected the truth, but his days spent at the Bluebonnet had taught him there were times when burying the truth was a kindness. And technically, it wasn't a lie. As far as he knew, Kyra's activities did not include carnally lying with any man.

Professor Hadley frowned, his eyes bloodshot and unfocused. "Don't be a fool, Mr. Kent. I found her diary at home. She came here to be a whore." Hadley yanked Kyra closer to his side, and she whimpered.

"I've slept with no one, for payment or otherwise," Kyra said, trying to pull out of her husband's grip, but despite his inebriation, he held tight.

"At least she's barren, so there will be no bastard child." Hadley laughed harshly.

The professor's cruel words hit Declan like a physical blow. Before he could think, his fist was flying, connecting with Hadley's jaw with a sickening crunch. The man crumpled to the floor, out cold, and the patrons erupted in gasps and cheers, the drunken crowd enjoying the entertainment.

Kyra stared at Declan in shock, the back of her hand pressed to her mouth. "What have you done?" she whispered, her voice trembling as she knelt beside her unmoving husband.

Declan flexed his throbbing hand, his chest heaving with barely contained rage. "No man should ever speak to you like that," he said, his tone low and fierce.

"You spoke to me like that," Kyra said, her gaze slicing into him like a knife.

"I never spoke such hateful words, Miss Bailey," Declan said.

She shook her head, her chin quivering. "All men are hateful."

Declan's heart cracked at the despair in her words. He reached out, cupping her face gently in his hands. "Not all men, Kyra. Not like that."

For a moment, they simply stared at each other. "Why are you being kind? Is it guilt for what we've done?" Kyra whispered, her eyes searching his.

"I was wrong, and I admit that I was wrong for how I've treated you in the past," Declan said fiercely. "I'll be damned if I let anyone treat you as anything less than a lady."

"Even if I'm a whore?" Kyra's eyes bored into his, challenging him.

"Even then."

A flicker of hope rose in her eyes, but reality came crashing back as Professor Hadley stirred on the floor, groaning in pain, and Declan reluctantly stepped away from Kyra.

"He'll never let me go." Kyra shook her head, defeated. "I was a fool to believe I could be free from him."

"Get him up," Declan ordered Jacob, who'd been hovering nearby. "Bring him to his room to sleep it off. And make sure he doesn't come near Miss Bailey."

As the professor was hauled away, Declan turned back to Kyra. "Will you be alright?" he asked.

"You shouldn't have done that," she said, straightening her skirt. "Henry will be furious."

"I can handle him," Declan said.

"As can I. I've endured much worse from a man," she said

pointedly, and Declan cringed, knowing she referred to things he'd said to her. But he'd never physically harm her.

"Again. I regret my earlier words. Please forgive me, Kyra."

"Your kindness is more unsettling than your cutting insults," Kyra said, but the corner of her mouth hitched into a sad smile. "I appreciate what you've done for me. No man has ever stood up for me."

Kyra exhaled a long breath. "But I'm still his wife. Nothing can change that."

With those words, she turned and walked up the stairs, her skirts swishing around her legs. Declan clenched his jaw, fighting the overwhelming desire to follow her. Instead, he stalked out of the saloon into the muggy Texas twilight.

The pungent scent of horses and dust filled his lungs. The sun was just sinking below the horizon, painting the open sky in streaks of orange and pink. He claimed Blaze from the hotel stables and swung up into the saddle. He kicked the horse into a gallop and raced down the empty dirt road out of town, away from Kyra and his tangled feelings.

2 4

───

DECLAN

The wind whipped at Declan's face as he urged the mustang faster, his mind churning. Over the short time he'd known her, his feelings for Kyra had transformed from annoyance to affection. One minute he was locking her in her room, chiding her for being a whore, and the next, he was filled with shame for how he'd treated her.

If he could, he'd take back every harmful word he'd uttered to her. He never thought he'd like a woman like Kyra—sharp-witted with a fierce spirit. Yes, his pulse had always quickened when her stormy gray eyes locked with his, but he'd mistaken the flutter in his chest for loathing. Now he realized there'd always been an undeniable attraction lurking under the surface, like two magnets whose opposites had pushed each other away until his flipped. If only she felt that way too, but it was obvious she didn't have the same yearnings. And then there was the little issue of her being married.

He shoved his new Stetson down on his head and kicked Blaze's flank, commanding the horse to move faster. The need to protect Kyra had embedded itself deep in his bones, and he wanted it gone. It wasn't his job to protect her. She wasn't his.

But he'd never forgive himself if harm came to her, especially from her own husband.

He rode Blaze hard, and by the time they returned, they were both in desperate need of water. Declan stabled Blaze and watered the horse, grooming him and settling him into his stall.

The town was hushed; only the sounds of coyotes yapping echoed beyond the squat buildings of the sleepy town as he walked down Main Street. The lights were dimmed at the Bluebonnet Hotel, the saloon open but solemn. How long had he been riding? His stomach lurched. What if something had happened to Kyra in his absence? What if Hadley had escaped his room and harmed her?

Declan rushed into the deserted lobby and found Scarlett perched on the front desk, a knowing grin marring her painted face.

"She's fine," she said, somehow understanding the meaning behind his desperation. "Asleep in her room, and Jacob's outside Henry's room." Scarlett tapped her long nails on the worn wood.

"Henry is going to be trouble," she said. "For us and for Kyra. We need to get rid of him."

"Kill him?" Declan asked, horrified.

Scarlett bent over laughing. "Nothing that drastic," she said once she'd recovered.

Declan rested his hat on the desk and ran a hand through his matted hair. "How do you mean?"

Scarlett grinned slyly. "He loves his booze, as you've seen. Let's ply him with liquor and women and, when he's good and drunk, make him sign a contract of divorce."

"It takes time to get a divorce. And it would need to be filed through the courts in Maine. And I doubt he'll be tempted by wanton flesh."

"Men may want their wives to be saints, but they have no problem bedding a whore." Scarlett slid off the desk. "I'll take care of the divorce contract. I'm friendly with the town's solicitor. It may take a few days, so we'll need him distracted until then."

Declan snorted skeptically. "You think he'll really sign it? He may be a drunk, but he's clever."

"It's the best plan I've got." Scarlett shrugged.

Though he didn't entirely approve of Scarlett's manipulations, Declan couldn't deny it was their best option, and he grudgingly agreed.

"Have one of the girls—Jewell—charm him tomorrow," Declan instructed. "Keep him away from Miss Bailey."

"Well, look at you playing the part of a ruthless businessman," Scarlett teased. "I knew you weren't as straitlaced as you pretended."

Declan glowered at her, refusing to admit there was a shred of truth in her words. "I'm trying to keep my investment intact. The sooner this mess between Professor Hadley and Miss Bailey is settled, the better for the sale of this place."

"Any nibbles from buyers?" Scarlett asked, gathering empty glasses from around the lobby, walking them into the saloon, and placing them on the bar to be washed later.

"A few bites," Declan said. "One of the potential buyers has been delayed but should be arriving this week, and I'd like the professor gone by then."

Scarlett frowned. "If the buyer comes early, we may need to make Henry scarce for a day or two."

"And how would you do that?" Declan frowned.

"Men get lost around here all the time. You could encourage him to go for a ride with you and then, *oops* ... leave him behind."

Declan scowled. "That sounds dangerous."

"Oh, he won't really be alone. I'll pay one of the Cherokees to keep an eye on him, unseen. If he's in any real danger, the Indian will come to his rescue."

"You keep interesting company, Scarlett."

"I keep the company that's needed." She smiled.

Bidding Scarlett goodnight, Declan lumbered upstairs, his body heavy with exhaustion, his thighs sore from his ride. He went straight to Hadley's room and glanced in. The man was crumpled on the bed, snoring loudly.

"Make sure he doesn't leave this room," Declan said to Jacob, who sat in a chair outside the door.

Next, he made his way to Kyra's room and paused at her door, straining to hear any sounds from within. He rested his palm on the solid wood, imagining he could feel the warmth of her presence on the other side.

In that moment, he made a vow. No matter what it took, he would find a way to free Kyra from the chains of her miserable marriage. He had his doubts about Scarlett's plan. A divorce was not as straightforward as she seemed to believe.

In the morning, he'd look into the laws of divorce in Maine and if it was a viable solution. He'd also tell Kyra of the plan. He wouldn't keep what they were doing a secret from her. It was her marriage, her life. She'd obviously come here for an escape, but minds change.

Kyra deserved a chance at happiness, and he'd be damned if he didn't fight to give it to her. But if she believed her happiness was back with her husband, he would not prevent it.

Swallowing the bitter ache in his chest, Declan took his hand from her door and walked away.

25

KYRA

Kyra awoke to a sharp knock on her door, the sound pulling her from a night of tossing and turning. She rolled onto her back, staring up at the discolored ceiling as memories of the previous night flooded her mind—Henry's drunken rage, Declan's fierce protectiveness, his use of her Christian name. It all felt like a dream, strange and unsettling.

The knock came again. Was it Henry, demanding she pack her things and leave? Kyra took a deep breath, steeled herself for whatever awaited her on the other side, and yanked the door open.

Declan stood before her, his broad shoulders filling the door-frame. Kyra blinked, taking in his appearance. His face was more tanned than when he'd first arrived, and to her surprise, he hadn't shaved. It was a first, even after she'd broken his razor in a fit of annoyance that first day.

He looked off-kilter, his eyes shadowed with weariness. His gaze dropped to her chest, and then he quickly looked away. She wore a loose-fitting slip that scooped low, nearly exposing her nipples.

"Don't you think we're past being bashful?" Kyra said, despite her fatigue. "You have seen me with my skirts—"

"Let us forget all that," Declan said, cutting her off.

"Of course." Her cheeks flared red, embarrassed that he wanted to forget their intimate moment. "How are you faring this morning?"

He cleared his throat, his gaze flickering away from her chest. "Everything is well."

His formal tone set her on edge.

"What do you want?" she asked, crossing her arms.

Declan's light eyes darkened. "It's about your husband."

Kyra groaned. She shuffled to the chair where her blue dress from the day before hung and slipped it over her head. "I must have my morning coffee if we're to have this conversation."

He nodded stiffly. "Of course. I'll fetch some now."

Unease churned in her stomach. Her husband's presence had thrown a wrench into everything, including the spark she swore had been ignited between Declan and herself.

A few minutes later, Declan arrived with a steaming pot of coffee and a plate of biscuits and jam. He poured them both a cup, and Kyra took a sip, letting the bitter liquid warm her tongue.

Declan ignored his cup, his hands clasped behind his back, as handsome as ever, even with a scowl. Kyra's heart stumbled in her chest. How had she not seen it before? Was it because they could no longer be together? Declan had become the proverbial forbidden fruit, and Kyra wanted to take a bite badly.

"I realize this has all been very unexpected," she said, turning away from Declan, unable to look at him, "But you need not worry. I shall be leaving with him today."

"What? Why?" he asked, his voice faltering.

"Because he's my husband," Kyra said, hating the words even as she spoke them. "And because his presence here could cause issues for the other girls. If he continues to make scenes, to accuse me publicly of being unfaithful and whoring, it could ruin the hotel's reputation. The longer he stays, the more chance there is of him discovering what transpired between me and…" Kyra faltered, unable to mention their intimate acts. Instead, she finished, "the sheriff."

Kyra's cheeks burned at her mention of the tryst with Sheriff Mack. It was no secret to Declan, but her stomach clenched with betrayal as she spoke to him about being with another man.

"I don't want to, but I have to," Kyra whispered, her voice catching.

"Scarlett and I have a plan," Declan said in a rush of urgency.

He explained the plan, and excitement churned in Kyra's belly. But so did fear.

"I doubt it will be that easy. And Henry's no fool." Kyra crossed her arms, protecting her heart. "What if he discovers our deception?"

"We must try. Don't you agree?"

"Yes, but if it doesn't work, that's it. I shall depart with him. Fighting him will only make things worse for you. You said so yourself."

Kyra searched Declan's face for some sign of the man who had vehemently apologized the night before, who she swore had changed his fury at her to something softer. But all she saw was a cool, distant stranger.

"I'll go ahead with your plan—as desperate as it is," she said. "If that is what you wish."

Declan's jaw tightened, a muscle pulsing in his cheek. "It's about you and your husband. What I want is irrelevant."

"Everything you've done to me since I arrived has been about what you want," she said, anger rising in her, hot and sharp. "You should be happy for me to accept my fate as a good, obedient wife."

"That's not what I want for you, Kyra," Declan said, and her stomach flip-flopped at his use of her name. "But if this plan doesn't work out, I fear for your safety."

"I'm not scared," Kyra said, tears burning her eyes, very much afraid. "I came here for my happiness and a life of freedom. And now I may be doomed to misery."

Declan closed his eyes in a long blink. "Then this plan must work, Miss Bailey."

"What happened to Kyra?"

"What do you mean?" he asked, alarm in his eyes.

"You just called me Kyra, and now I'm back to Miss Bailey."

"Do you prefer your Christian name?" he asked.

"From you, yes."

Declan stared at her, his gaze filled with care. But as quick as it came, the softness hardened. "With your marriage uncertain, I think it best we keep our relationship formal."

Kyra felt as if the ground had dropped out from beneath her feet. He was right, but it still hurt.

"Then go," she whispered, her voice shaking. "We should keep our distance."

He exhaled a tortured breath, his eyes full of anguish. But he didn't argue, didn't try to persuade her. "As you wish, Miss Bailey." Then he turned and walked out of her room.

Kyra had thought the Bluebonnet would be her sanctuary, a place where she could finally be free. She still believed it could be.

She didn't know what the future held, didn't know if she had the strength to face it. But one thing was certain: she would not let anyone—not her husband, not Declan, not even her own fears —decide her fate.

She was done being a pawn in other people's games.

26

KYRA

Kyra marched to the other side of the hotel to Henry's room, her heart racing in her chest. The sun shone hot and stifling through the windows—the Texas heat oppressive and humid—but it was nothing compared to the raging turmoil pumping through her veins.

She had spent the morning in a fitful rage, her stomach sour with dread, doubting Scarlett's plan to trick Henry into signing a generous divorce agreement in Kyra's favor.

Kyra was well-read on the laws around divorce. For instance, she knew that Maine was more liberal than most states when it came to divorce, especially for women. Legally, she could file for divorce based on Henry's excessive drunkenness or his acts of adultery. The problem was she had no evidence.

None of Henry's friends or colleagues would speak out against him regarding his drinking. He hid it well. And she had no proof of his adultery, only suspicion. If she'd believed filing for divorce on those grounds was a viable course of action, she would've done that instead of abandoning her marriage and running off to Texas, which may have been shortsighted on her part, as the courts looked down upon the spouse who abandoned the marriage.

Texas law was even less forgiving.

Kyra needed to face Henry, to find out what he truly wanted from her, because she didn't believe he'd come all this way just to drag her back to their miserable life in Maine. All he ever wanted was Betty, and she was a widow, free to be his. It made no sense that he'd fight this hard to stay married to Kyra.

Taking a deep breath, Kyra pushed his door open, but his room was empty. Her shoulders sank, guessing where he might be.

In the saloon, the dim interior matched her mood. She spotted Henry sitting at a table tucked in the corner, a nearly empty glass of whiskey in front of him.

"Henry," she said, approaching him cautiously. "Let's talk."

He looked up at her, his eyes bloodshot and his face unshaven. "So, the prodigal wife returns," he sneered. "Come to beg for my forgiveness?"

Kyra gritted her teeth, refusing to be cowed by his disdain. "I want to know what you're really doing here. I know it's not because you missed me."

He leaned back in his chair, a sad smile playing on his lips, but kept silent.

"You never wanted to marry me," she whispered, her voice shaky. "You only did it because of the baby. Why can't you let this sham of a marriage go? Why come all this way to drag me back?"

Henry's eyes narrowed, and he glared into his empty glass. "Because I can't have a wife who's a whore, Kyra. Betty won't allow it. It would ruin my reputation, my standing at the college. I could lose my job."

Anger surged through her veins, but with a tinge of hope. "So, you'll divorce me, but only if I come back with you pure as the driven snow? Is that it?"

"And promise never to return here, even after the divorce.

And you'll get nothing from me—no alimony, no division of property. I'll need it in writing in the divorce contract." He refilled his glass with the whiskey bottle that sat on the table. "It seems I've come just in time, before you could completely besmirch my name with your wanton behavior."

Kyra closed her eyes, trapping the tears that threatened to fall. She'd dreamed of a life free from the chains of her marriage, but even in divorce, she'd be tethered to Henry's rules.

"No," she said, using the only hand she could play. "I'll divorce you, but once the papers are signed, I'll make my own choices. I'll play the dutiful divorcée until you remarry, but then my life will be on my own terms."

Henry laughed, the sound harsh and mocking. "Do you really think I'd agree to that? You'll come back here. You'll be a pariah, a fallen woman. And I'll still be ruined. The divorce itself will leave me on tenterhooks."

Kyra lifted her chin, meeting his gaze with defiance. "Think about my offer, Henry, or you'll never be with Betty."

She turned on her heel, striding out of the saloon into the blazing sun. As soon as the doors swung shut behind her, she ran. She found respite in the cool stables and collapsed against the low wall of one of the stalls, her breath coming in ragged gasps.

"Miss Bailey," a deep voice said above her. "What's happened? Are you injured?"

Declan, sweaty from exercising his horse, held the reins of Blaze. His shirtsleeves were rolled up and revealed his tanned, muscular forearms. At the sight of him, her pulse raced and her mouth wetted.

Kyra swallowed hard, her tongue darting out to moisten her suddenly dry lips. "Henry's agreed to divorce me, but only if I return with him and never come back here."

Declan's eyes widened with alarm. "And you've agreed?"

"I've told him I won't divorce him if those are his terms. But I may have no choice. I tried to reason with him, to threaten, but nothing worked."

His eyes shadowed. "We still have the original plan. Make him stupid on drink and get him to sign a contract to your liking. Tempt him with women when he's out of his mind, then blackmail him if he makes trouble."

"We wouldn't even need to blackmail him," Kyra said without conviction. "With enough witnesses, I'd have the legal right to a divorce. But Henry would see this coming, and he won't do anything to put the power back in my hands. He knows the law as well as I."

"We must try," he said, his voice low and fierce. He took a step closer, his broad shoulders looming, a shadow of determination in his gaze. "You must fight, Kyra. You've come too far to give up now."

She clutched the coarse wood of the stall behind her, her knuckles whitening as she wrestled with the urge to collapse into him. The raw conviction in his voice calmed her battered nerves.

"And we must do it soon," Declan said. "I received word this morning that my brother's trial starts in just a few days."

"Declan," she murmured, an ache in her voice. "You've sacrificed so much for him."

He shook his head, a mirthless laugh escaping his lips. "What kind of man would I be if I didn't? He's my brother, Kyra. My responsibility." His gaze locked with hers, and in that moment, she could see every crack in his armor—the weariness, the pain, the burden of being the one who always had to stand strong. He often infuriated her, but in these quiet moments, she saw the real Declan Kent.

"You've done more than any man should be expected to do," she said, her fingers brushing against his arm.

"I'm trying, Kyra," he said, his voice barely above a whisper. "But some days, I wonder if it's enough."

"It is," she said, stepping closer, drawn to him like a horse to the trough.

Their eyes met, and the world around them dissolved, leaving only the fragile, electric connection that tethered them together. Declan reached up, his calloused fingers brushing a strand of hair from her face, lingering at her temple. The rough warmth of his touch sent shivers cascading down her spine.

"Kyra," he breathed, her name a prayer, a plea, and a warning all at once.

She closed her eyes, her breath catching as the space between them disappeared. His forehead rested against hers, his hand slipping to cup her cheek, holding her as though she might shatter if he let go.

"I don't want to leave," he murmured, his lips so close she could feel the whisper of his breath against her skin.

Her heart thundered, every rational thought drowned out. His gaze dropped to her mouth, his breath hitching, and she leaned in ever so slightly, her heart aching with a longing so fierce it might consume her. But then, just as the precipice loomed close, Declan pulled back, his hand falling away.

"I should go," she said, the words daggers in her throat.

"Yes," he replied hoarsely, turning away. "You should."

She hesitated, wanting to say something—anything—to bridge the chasm that had opened between them. But no words came, only the heavy silence of everything left unsaid.

At the door, she paused, glancing back at him. "If our plan fails and I have to go," she said, "I'll miss you, Declan Kent."

"Then let's make sure it doesn't fail," he replied, a shadow of a smile tugging at his lips.

She stepped out into the clawing summer heat, her heart full of a bittersweet longing, the future she'd dreamed of slipping away.

Chapter 27 Declan

Declan stood in the dimly lit saloon, his eyes scanning the raucous crowd. The air was thick with cigar smoke and the scent of cheap liquor, and the cacophony of drunken laughter and clinking glasses filled the room. He spotted Bryan hovering near Henry's table, diligently keeping Henry's glass full, just as they'd planned.

Henry slumped in his chair, his face flushed and his words slurred as he hurled insults at Mei and Jewell. But the girls played their parts to perfection, giggling and flirting, unfazed by his crude remarks.

With a deep breath, Declan caught Kyra's eye and nodded toward his office. She followed him, her skirts rustling softly as they made their way through the crowded room.

Inside the office, Scarlett waited, the freshly drawn contract from the town's solicitor spread out on the desk. To Declan's surprise, Kyra had been quite knowledgeable about what needed to be done for the contract. Kyra was smart, but he hadn't realized she understood the law so clearly.

Declan's heart raced as he pointed to a line at the bottom of the document. "Sign here. As a notary, I can witness the signatures."

It was a perfect trap, if it worked. Kyra had explained that the document wouldn't be legal if it were proven Henry signed it when he was intoxicated, but she had listed chronic drunkenness as one of her reasons for filing for divorce. So, if Henry admitted he was drunk when he signed the document, he'd be admitting in a legal proceeding that he drank to the point of drunkenness, and she could make a new filing with that as evidence.

With shaking hands, Kyra took the pen Declan offered and signed her name. As he stamped the document, Declan fought to keep his expression neutral, even as his heart soared with the possibility of Kyra's freedom.

"Now," Scarlett said, her voice low and conspiratorial, "we

need to get Henry to sign. He's in quite a state, so hopefully it'll be easy."

"I've got this." Declan folded up the document and tucked it in his jacket as they made their way to the saloon.

Declan's plan was to first show Henry his hotel bill and bar tab and tell him that the hotel would cover all debts since they unknowingly hosted a married woman. Then Declan would ask Henry to sign the bill, confirming all payments were null and void. But at the last moment, Declan would trade out the hotel bill for the signature page of the divorce contract, hoping Henry, in his inebriated state, wouldn't look too closely.

Henry could contest it once he realized he'd been tricked, but Declan prayed Kyra was correct and that Henry would never admit legally that he was drunk.

At Henry's small table, Jewell perched on Henry's lap, her arms draped around his neck.

With a sudden, violent movement, he shoved her away. "You're not my Betty," he slurred, his voice thick with drunken anger. "I'll only ever touch Betty. Even when I'm with Kyra, I'm thinking of Betty. Her lips, her skin, her chestnut hair..."

Kyra stiffened beside him, pain flashing across her face. Fury rose in his chest, but he forced it down, reminding himself of their goal. Gently, he ushered Mei and Jewell away from the table.

"Professor Hadley," Declan said, keeping his voice businesslike, "since you and Miss Bailey are leaving tomorrow, I need you to sign this letter. It states that I've taken care of all your debts during your stay here."

Henry squinted at the paper with the itemized bill, his eyes struggling to focus. After a moment, he shrugged and held out his hand.

"Pen," he demanded.

With a silent prayer, Declan discreetly switched out the page and handed Henry the pen. Henry scrawled his signature across the bottom, the ink bleeding into the paper where he pressed too hard.

A collective sigh of relief passed through the group when he dropped the pen, the deed done. Declan reached for the paper, but Henry shakily stood, blocking him momentarily.

"To bed," Henry said, swaying. His leg caught the edge of the table and it tipped, wobbling on its legs, and sent the glass of whiskey cascading across the contract. The amber liquid seeped into the paper, smearing the ink until the words and signatures became an unintelligible mess. Kyra let out a small, choked sob, reaching for the paper, but it was too late. The signature was obliterated, the contract ruined.

Henry chuckled. "Write up another bill tomorrow, Mr. Kent. I'll sign it in the morning." With that, he staggered toward the stairs, leaving a trail of destruction in his wake.

Declan stared at the useless contract, his heart sinking. Beside him, Kyra picked up the dripping mess, the ink sliding down the page.

"The solicitor's left town," Scarlett murmured, her voice heavy with disappointment. "He won't be back for two days."

"And we'll be gone tomorrow," Kyra whispered, crumpling the paper in her hand, their plan ruined in a matter of seconds.

Declan took a step toward Kyra and placed a hand gently on her arm, pulling her away from the noise. "We'll figure something out," he said. "There has to be another way."

But Kyra shook her head, tears dripping down her cheeks. "It's useless, Declan."

The words hit Declan like a physical blow. "But—"

"No," Kyra spoke vehemently. "I have to accept my fate with Henry."

"Please, Kyra." Declan snatched her hands, pleading. "There must be something. I can't lose—"

Kyra pulled out of his grip, wiping her tears roughly. "If you care for me, you'll let me go."

He wanted to argue, to insist that they could find a solution, but the hopelessness in Kyra's eyes silenced him.

"I must depart tomorrow for Frisco," he said, his voice rough with suppressed emotion. "Or I'd chase that solicitor down."

Kyra nodded, resigned. "And soon you'll be gone too. Back in Kentucky."

They stood there for a moment, the air between them heavy with unspoken words. Hell, he'd say them all if Kyra hadn't made it clear she wanted to hear none of them from him. She'd never indicated she shared any affection for Declan besides gratitude. Still, Declan's heart ached to pull her close, to tell her how he felt, to beg her not to go. But the words remained trapped in his throat, held back by fear and propriety and the cruel twist of fate that had brought them to this moment.

"Well," Kyra said at last, her voice barely above a whisper, "I suppose this is goodbye, then."

Declan nodded stiffly, his jaw clenched against the tide of emotion threatening to overwhelm him. "I suppose it is. Farewell, Kyra. I wish you all the best."

She looked up at him, her eyes shimmering. For a moment, Declan thought she might give voice to feelings he hoped she possessed for him, but she simply nodded, turned, and walked away.

Declan watched her go, his heart cracking piece by piece. He wanted to call out to her, to run after her and tell her he needed her, that he couldn't bear the thought of her leaving. But he remained rooted to the spot, his hands clenched at his sides, as she walked out of the saloon and into the hotel toward her room.

As the saloon door shut behind her, Declan's heart went black. He knew, with a certainty that shook him to his core, that he would never be the same again. No matter where life took him, a part of his heart would always belong to Kyra.

DECLAN

The next morning, before the sun rose, Declan readied Blaze and rode to the small town of Frisco. He'd said farewell to Kyra the night before, and he couldn't do it again. He didn't think his heart could handle it.

How strange to have been with Kyra in so many intimate ways, and yet he'd never kissed her. The regret of what could've been wrapped around him like a lasso, but halfway to Frisco, he could no longer take it. He had to make a choice. Kyra was the past, and he must look toward the future. Not an easy task with her wrapped up in his heart, but he must try.

The weight of the upcoming trial hung heavy in his body. This time next week, his brother could be hanging from a rope. Shooting a sheriff's deputy was not taken lightly, and the deputy was out for blood, determined to see Clive pay the full cost for what he claimed was a deliberate attempt on his life.

As Declan dismounted his horse and tied Blaze to the hitching post, a sense of dread washed over him. This time, Declan feared that even he wouldn't be able to save his brother.

He opened the creaking door of the sheriff's office and

stepped inside the dark and humid room. The older man sat at his desk, pulling papers from a drawer.

"Sheriff Adler," Declan said, breathless from his long ride.

"You made it, Mr. Kent." The sheriff took his hat from the peg beside the door and ushered Declan out into the steamy air. "They moved the trial up. It began a few minutes ago. Come."

Declan rushed after Sheriff Adler, his heart pounding. Thank God he came today. Trials typically lasted one day. On rare occasions, they could go for a few days, but not a trial like Clive's. It should be over in a matter of hours.

The small courtroom was hot and stuffy, the air thick with the smell of sweat and dust. Declan took a seat behind Clive, who sat slumped at the defendant's table, his face pale and drawn.

The lawyer Declan had hired, a man named Jeremiah Stevens, stood beside him, shuffling through a stack of papers. The prosecutor, a stern-faced man named Philip Thompson, stood to speak, calling his first witness.

Deputy Elias Woods took the stand, his arm in a sling and his face twisted with anger.

"Deputy Woods, can you please tell the court what happened on the night of May fifteenth?" Thompson asked, his voice ringing out in the silent courtroom.

Elias nodded, his eyes fixed on Clive. "I was at the local saloon in town, having a drink as one does after a long day. I was at a table behind the sheriff and several locals. They had piled all their hats atop the sheriff's head, betting someone to shoot the top one off. Now we all knew this was not a serious bet. Just a group of merry gentlemen letting off steam after a hard day's labor. But then that man"—Elias pointed a finger at Clive, his voice shaking with barely suppressed rage—"came stumbling toward the table, drunk as an alley cat, swinging his gun, swearing and cursing, and up to no good."

Declan's hands clenched into fists at his sides. He knew that his brother could get mean and reckless when he was in his cups.

But he also knew that Clive would never intentionally harm anyone.

The defense lawyer, Stevens, stood up, his face calm and composed. "Objection, Your Honor. The witness is speculating as to my client's state of mind and intentions."

The judge, a grizzled old man with a bushy gray beard, nodded. "Sustained. The jury will disregard the witness's last statement regarding the defendant's state of mind."

Prosecutor Thompson scowled but continued. "What happened next, Deputy Woods?"

Elias took a deep breath, his eyes never leaving Clive's face. "He kept waving that gun around, saying he was ready for some fun and he'd shoot anyone who tried to stop him. That's when he took aim and..." He paused, his voice catching. "And shot me, right in the shoulder."

Declan's stomach twisted with dread. From what he'd been told, the deputy's story was close to the truth, but he doubted Clive made threats. Most likely, he got caught up in the fun of the game without realizing no one truly intended to shoot at the hats upon the sheriff's head.

Yes, Clive had been drunk that night, but the shooting had been an accident. He also knew that the law was the law. Clive had shot a deputy, accident or not.

Stevens stood up, his face grim. "Deputy Woods, did you see my client shoot you? Did you witness the bullet leaving the gun?"

Woods hesitated, his brow furrowing. "Yes. I saw it clear as day."

"Interesting. The saloon was crowded that night, with many patrons who were also armed and intoxicated, correct?"

Thompson jumped to his feet, his face flushed with anger. "Objection, Your Honor. The defense is leading the witness."

The judge waved a hand. "Overruled. The witness may answer."

Woods nodded reluctantly. "Yes, many were intoxicated. It's

the purpose of going to a bar, after all." There were chuckles from the few attendees in the courtroom. "And yes, most of them were armed, as any respectable man would be."

Stevens nodded. "So, it's possible that the bullet that struck you came from someone else's gun? Someone who is not my client?"

Woods's face twisted with fury. "No. It was him. I saw it clear as day."

"I see," Stevens said deliberately, glancing over his shoulder at two ladies sitting at the back of the court. "Because I have several witnesses who will claim that not only was the bar crowded to the brim, but you had been distracted by several of the ladies who are known to frequent the saloon looking for business."

"That's a lie!" Elias shot up from the stand, but the damage had been done.

The possible doubt of Elias as a reliable witness settled into the court and over the jurors' faces. Then Thompson called his final witness, a man named Seth Hawkins. Hawkins was a thin, weaselly-looking man with shifty eyes and a nervous twitch in his jaw. Declan immediately didn't trust him.

"Mr. Hawkins," Thompson said, his voice smooth and confident. "Can you please tell the court what you saw on the night of May fifteenth?"

Hawkins nodded, his eyes darting around the room. "I was in the saloon having a drink. I saw the defendant, Mr. Clive Kent, stumbling around as always. He was shouting and waving his gun around. And then I saw him point the gun right at the sheriff, who I believe was his original target, but he missed and hit the deputy's shoulder."

Declan's heart sank as several of the jurors shifted forward, listening intently. Before the defense could call their first witness, a clerk rushed into the courtroom and gave the judge a note. To Declan's surprise, the judge adjourned the trial until the next day, stating he had an urgent matter to attend to and they'd reconvene in the morning. Unusual, but not unheard of if the judge had other business.

As Declan stepped out of the small courthouse, a weight settled on his shoulders. He felt more defeated than ever. For the first time in his life, he felt truly alone—not because Clive was locked away or because his family was hundreds of miles from Wylde. No, the emptiness came from the absence of Miss Kyra Bailey.

In just a few weeks, he'd come to depend on her steady presence and her uncanny ability to lift his spirits, even in the darkest moments. The need for her had crept up on him, catching him unaware. When they first met, she'd been nothing short of infuriating. Now, every breath he took felt strained without her near.

Declan pushed down the sharp pain in his gut, a tangled knot of longing, sorrow, and the suffocating anxiety that had gripped him since Clive's arrest. The last few weeks had been a relentless storm, battering his every waking moment and threatening to tear him apart.

Declan forced himself to keep moving, his boots echoing hollowly against the uneven boards of the courthouse steps. The wind carried the distant hum of the town, indifferent to his turmoil.

At the sheriff's office, Declan found Clive sitting in his cramped cell, his face haggard and his eyes haunted.

"You should just let them hang me, Declan," Clive said, his voice flat. "I've always been a burden to you, always dragged you down with my mistakes."

Declan shook his head fiercely. "Shut your trap, Clive. There's still hope."

But even as he said the words, he knew they were empty. If the jury found Clive guilty, he could hang by the end of the week.

With a cold heart, Declan made his way to the telegraph office. He needed to let Scarlett know that he would be gone for another few days.

The message sent, Declan dragged himself to his small hotel room. Kyra would be gone by now, and for a brief moment, he wished he were the one hanging by the rope.

Ashamed at the thought, his head snapped up. Of course, he didn't wish death upon himself. But he longed for anything to take away the raw, all-consuming ache. Even if she'd stayed, there was no guarantee she cared for him.

A bitter longing pulsed in his chest. He faced the prospect of losing his brother and returning to an empty life without her. He didn't know which was more devastating.

28

KYRA

Kyra stood in the middle of her room at the Bluebonnet, her hands on her hips as she surveyed the scattered clothes and the few belongings she'd accumulated during her time there. With her heart heavy as stone, she packed, folding each item neatly and placing it into her nearly pristine satchel, for she and Henry had never traveled or had adventures.

She tried not to think about what awaited her back in Maine, back with Henry. He'd promised her a divorce if she returned with him, but at such a cost, she wondered if it would be worth it. If she wasn't allowed to come back to the Bluebonnet, how would she earn enough to make a reasonable living?

A knock at the door startled her from her depressing thoughts. She opened it, surprised to see Sheriff Mack standing there, his hat in his hands and a look of determination on his face.

"Sheriff," she said, her voice wary. "What can I do for you?"

He stepped into the room, his eyes scanning her body.

"I hear you're leaving today. Would you be so obliged as to

have one more turn about the bed before you go?" he asked, his voice low.

Kyra's heart sank. It had been thrilling when they'd been together previously, but the excitement had had nothing to do with him. It was the freedom and power it had given her. Now that felt like a lifetime ago.

"I'm sorry, Sheriff," she said, her voice firm. "I can't. I'm leaving on the late morning train, going back to Maine with my husband."

"It won't take long." He stepped closer, wrapping his arm around her waist gently. "I'll pay double, whatever you wish."

Before Kyra could respond, a voice rang out behind them in the doorway. "What in the heavens is going on?" She turned to see Henry, his face twisted with fury. "What are you doing in my wife's room, Sheriff?"

The sheriff stepped back and shrugged lazily. "Enjoying her company."

Kyra's heart raced at the danger of the situation. If Henry found out about her previous encounter with the sheriff, he'd use it against her, hold it over her head for the rest of her life.

"I think you should leave, Sheriff," she said, her voice calm and steady. "My husband and I will be leaving soon, and I need to finish packing."

But the sheriff stayed firm. "I'd make it worth your while if you stayed."

"How dare you!" Henry's voice rose. "My wife is no whore."

The sheriff laughed. "I beg to differ."

Kyra's mind raced as she tried to find a way out of the situation.

"How dare you," Henry said, puffing his chest out. "You may be the sheriff, but I can still have you arrested. Paying for carnal pleasure is a crime. I'll shut this place down. I'll turn it to dust."

Kyra's heart pounded as Henry's threat echoed in the room, his venomous words slicing through her. The Bluebonnet wasn't just a brothel to her; it was her salvation, her sanctuary, and the one place that had offered her a chance to rebuild her life after the wreckage she'd left behind.

Scarlett had built the Bluebonnet into a haven, a place where women could reshape their shattered lives, support their families, and reclaim a sense of dignity in a world that offered them little. Declan had risked everything to protect this place and the people who depended on it, overcoming his own misgivings.

Henry's threat wasn't just an attack on the Bluebonnet—it was an attack on everyone she'd come to care about. And Kyra couldn't let that happen. She wouldn't let that happen.

Rage surged through her, but it brought with it something unexpected: clarity. For too long, Henry had wielded his power over her, his influence over their lives, as if she were nothing more than a mistake he had to put up with. Now, she realized, she wasn't powerless.

Those hours spent sitting in on classes, listening to lectures on criminal law and procedure, weren't wasted moments. They were the foundation of a weapon she could wield. She had listened, absorbed, and learned that the law could be a tool—a means to an end if you understood how to bend it to your will. And Kyra understood. Oh, she understood.

"Henry," she said, her voice cutting through the tension like a razor, "you'd do well to tread carefully. You think you can threaten me, threaten this place, and walk away unscathed? Let me remind you—I know everything about you. I'm not the only one who has something to hide. You think I don't know about the students? The women you lured in over the years? And I assure you, Betty isn't the type to sully herself with the likes of you if she ever found out. I'm certain she'd be interested to hear what I have to say. As would the dean. As would your colleagues."

She watched as Henry's face blanched, the smug bravado draining from him in an instant. Power surged through her veins, a heady rush of strength she'd long forgotten she possessed.

"The law isn't just a sword, Henry," she added, her tone sharp and unwavering. "It's also a shield. And I'll use every bit of it to protect the Bluebonnet—and myself. So go ahead, puff your chest, make your threats. But remember this—I'm not the one with something to lose."

Henry's face turned red with anger, but Kyra pressed on. "Don't be angry, dear. I'm simply pointing out that we've all done things that are not right, things that we regret. I'm sure Betty would appreciate you being coolheaded in this matter and not ruining things for your future with her."

For a long moment, Henry simply stared at her, his jaw clenched in barely restrained rage.

"I think I'll leave you two to it," the sheriff said, his voice measured but firm. "This seems like a domestic matter. But don't try anything, sir. I've got friends in this town—savory and unsavory—and they don't take kindly to folks causing trouble." His gaze lingered on Henry, a silent warning, before he nodded at Kyra and exited, shutting the door behind him.

Kyra turned to Henry, his expression twisted with disgust.

"I won't divorce you," he said, his tone icy.

"How can you say that?" she demanded, forcing steel into her voice despite the tremor in her chest. "Those aren't empty threats, Henry. I have the law on my side."

"You won't do any of those things," he snapped, his lips curling into a bitter sneer. "I know you, Kyra. It's why you ran. If you were going to use those arguments against me, you'd have done it long ago. But you didn't. Instead, you fled like a coward, because deep down you know you'd lose."

Kyra's hands curled into fists, her nails biting into her palms. "I ran because I was drowning in grief, Henry! I couldn't think straight. I needed to escape the misery of being your wife. But now I have something to fight for—and I'm not afraid to stand up to you. Not anymore."

Henry's eyes narrowed, his voice dropping to a cold, cutting edge. "Fight all you want, Kyra. It doesn't change the fact that your sheriff has no pull beyond this nothing town. You humiliated me when you left. Do you have any idea the damage you caused? The whispers, the stares? If it weren't for my quick thinking, I'd have been a laughingstock in our social circle, a joke at the college. But I salvaged my reputation. I'm a respected professor. My word carries weight—much more than that of a wife who abandoned her marriage to become a whore."

The words hit Kyra like a slap, the cruelty of them stealing her breath. She saw it now—this wasn't about reason or love. It was about his ego. His threats weren't for reconciliation but to punish her for her defiance.

"You'll never have your precious Betty," she hissed, her voice trembling with fury. "I'll make sure of it."

She spun on her heel and stormed out of the room. Her vision blurred with tears as she descended the stairs, stumbling. She didn't know where she was going—only that she needed to get away, to find a moment to breathe, to think. But one thing was clear: Henry was more dangerous than she'd ever realized.

As she rounded the corner to the lobby, she nearly ran into Scarlett coming out of the office with a telegram in her hand.

"Kyra?" Scarlett said, her voice filled with concern. "What's wrong?"

Kyra shook her head, unable to speak. But then she noticed the name on the telegram, and her heart skipped a beat.

"Is that from Dec—Mr. Kent?" she asked, her voice barely above a whisper.

Scarlett nodded, her face grim. "The trial isn't going well," she said. "He'll be there a few more days. He's gravely concerned for his brother."

Kyra's mind raced. She thought of Declan, of the way he looked at her with a tenderness she'd never known before, certainly never from her husband.

"How far is Frisco?" she asked, a new determination filling her veins. She may not have won the war with Henry, but there was another battle worth fighting.

Scarlett's eyes widened in surprise. "Less than a half-day's ride."

With or without a promise of divorce, her life in Maine was over. Once he'd calmed down, she prayed Henry's love for Betty would win out over his ego and he'd eventually grant Kyra the divorce.

"May I have my wages? I want to go to Frisco for a few days. I can't stay here a minute longer, and I believe I can be of help to Declan."

Scarlett blinked several times, as if she couldn't process Kyra's words. Kyra could hardly believe what she was saying either.

Spewing out all that legal knowledge to Henry upstairs made her realize she might be of use to Declan and his brother's dire situation. The law had always intrigued her, but it had been a hobby. It never crossed her mind she could put it to good use.

Or maybe it had nothing to do with swooping in and saving the day and everything to do with her desperately wanting to see Declan Kent.

"But what about Henry? What about the divorce?"

Kyra shook her head. "Henry can do whatever he wants," she said, her voice hard. "I'm never going back to Maine. I'll move to Sioux Falls if I have to and get the divorce myself. I may be crazy, but being reasonable has never gotten me anything but misery. I was crazy when I made this journey here, and I've never felt so alive."

Scarlett's face broke into a wide grin. "Kyra, my dear," she said, her voice filled with satisfaction. "I don't think I've ever been prouder to call you my niece."

29

DECLAN

Declan sat in the dimly lit bar, his body aching with worry. He had gone there to drink away his troubles, to try and forget about the trial that was slithering away from them. His brother's fate would be decided the next day, and the thought of losing him—on top of Kyra—was too much to bear.

How would he tell his mother? His sister? It would break their hearts. His own heart was already breaking.

A commotion pulled him from his ruminations. Curious, he set his drink down and pushed the door open, stepping out into the hot night air. He stopped short, sure he saw a mirage.

Kyra Bailey stood before him, worn and tired, her hair disheveled and her dress covered in dust, much like she'd appeared the first time he'd seen her. She'd never looked more beautiful.

"Kyra?" he said, his voice barely above a whisper. "What are you doing here?"

She looked up at him, not with love but with fierce determination. "I'm here to help. Scarlett told me your brother's trial isn't going well, and I can't just stand by and do nothing."

"What about Henry?" Declan asked.

"Henry is more horrible than I ever imagined—a wounded animal lashing out. But he's of no concern to me anymore. I'm done letting him control my fate."

Declan's heart shoved into his throat. "You left him?"

Kyra's determined expression faltered. "I ... I think so. But that isn't why I've come. I may be able to help. Or, at least, I hope I can."

Declan shook his head. "I appreciate this, Kyra, but I'm afraid there's not much you can do. This is a matter for the courts, and as a woman—"

Kyra cut him off, her voice sharp and clear. "Don't you dare. My brain is made up of the same matter as yours. When I ran into Scarlett with your telegram, it hit me like a freight train. I know the law—better than you do. So let me be of use. Please."

"Kyra, you're mad," he said, his voice filled with wonder. "But we need a bit of madness right now."

"I'm tired of being reasonable." She smiled with a hint of wickedness.

They made their way to the small hotel where Declan was staying, and he insisted on paying for her accommodation. Then he escorted her to her small room but did not cross the threshold.

As they stood in the dim hallway, Declan stared into Kyra's stormy gray eyes, still unable to fully believe she was there. The faint lamplight caught the silvery glint of unshed tears in her gaze, making her look both fierce and fragile. His chest tightened with the overwhelming urge to pull her into his arms, to kiss her until the lines of pain and anger on her face melted away. But Kyra stood stiffly, her shoulders squared and her hands clenched at her sides.

He tried to convince himself that her wild gesture—rushing here, defending his brother—had everything to do with him. But it wasn't true. She wasn't there because of any deep feelings for

Declan. No, it was about a need to escape, her desperation to wrest control of her life from a man who'd twisted it into something hopeless for years.

Even so, the hope flickered, a stubborn flame he couldn't quite extinguish. He'd seen the way she looked at him sometimes, her gaze softening. He'd caught the way her breath hitched when they stood too close. Did she feel it too? This ache, this pull between them?

Declan took a tentative step closer, his heart pounding. "Kyra," he said, his voice low and uncertain. "I'm glad you're here." His fingers itched to reach out, to brush against her skin, but he kept his hands at his sides.

"I'm happy to help," she said, but her chin quivered, and she quickly looked away.

Unable to resist, he cupped her cheek, tilting her face back toward his. Her skin was warm beneath his touch, and her gray eyes met his, wide and uncertain. For a breathless moment, the space between them seemed to shrink. Her lips parted slightly, and his heart leapt.

But Kyra turned away, breaking the contact, and stepped back out of his reach.

"Goodnight, Declan," she murmured, her voice barely above a whisper. She didn't look at him as she turned and walked into her room.

Declan stood frozen, his hand still hovering in the air where her face had been moments before. The ache pressed like a weight against his heart, threatening to crush him as he watched her disappear, closing the door softly behind her.

For a long moment, he just stared at the empty space she'd left behind, his heart splintering under the weight of realization.

Damn it all. Why did he have to fall for a woman who so clearly didn't share the same tenderness for him?

His shields had been down too long. He'd allowed himself to dream of a future where Kyra might look at him the way he looked at her. But that night, the small, stubborn flame of hope flickered out.

Declan drew in a ragged breath, forcing himself to straighten. Hope was useless—it left him too exposed, too vulnerable. He had no choice but to lock his heart away again, to protect what little remained.

~

THE NEXT MORNING, they arrived at the courthouse together, Kyra looking smart in a forest-green dress and matching hat, freshly bathed that morning. Declan filled Kyra in on the details of the previous day's events, the witnesses, and the evidence he could recall. She'd listened intently, and as they took their seats behind Clive and his lawyer, he introduced Kyra.

"Pardon me, sir. But are you planning on calling the sheriff to the stand?" Kyra asked.

Mr. Stevens's eyes widened in surprise. "Excuse me?"

"It's just he was allegedly the intended target, correct?"

"Yes," he said, looking curiously at Kyra.

"Is he a witness for the defense?" she asked.

Mr. Stevens glanced at Declan.

"Her husband's a professor at a college up north. She used her spare time there learning about the law," Declan explained in response to Stevens's unasked question.

"The law has always fascinated me," Kyra explained, unapologetic. "So, has he been called to the stand as a witness for the defense?"

"No," Stevens said, sitting back in his chair, looking amused but not offended by her questions.

"Mr. Kent, from what you've told me, the sheriff isn't happy about this trial," Kyra said. "If you put him on the stand, do you think the sheriff would contradict that witness you mentioned to me? Seth Hawkins? It would give the jury reasonable doubt."

"Perhaps," Stevens said, looking over at Clive. "But he's on the defense's list, which would lead me to believe he would not speak in our favor."

"He hates Eli," Clive said with a bite. "I hear them fighting every day from my cell. And then the sheriff comes and lets off steam to me in the back when he's had enough of Eli."

"That might explain why he was never called," Stevens said, running his hand over his short beard. "He'd be their strongest witness, so it is suspect."

Sheriff Adler stood in the back of the courtroom, and Stevens and Declan walked over to him. For the first time in days, a sliver of hope snuck into Declan.

"Excuse me, Sheriff," Stevens said in a low whisper. "If you were called to the stand and asked what your recollection was of that night, what would you say?"

The sheriff smiled coyly. "Exactly what I told the prosecutor— that I don't recall seeing Clive shoot his gun that night. That there were several men joking about shooting those hats off my head. That it could've been any one of them."

Adrenaline shot through Declan, and he had to clamp his jaw shut to keep from hollering in joy. This could change everything.

"You're not pulling my leg, sir?" Stevens asked, a barely contained smile on his face.

"He listed me as a witness before he spoke to me, assuming I'd confirm Eli's story," the sheriff said.

"If I put you on the stand today, would you say the same thing you just said to me now?"

There was a glint of mischief in Sheriff Adler's eyes as he said, "Damn straight."

30

KYRA

"In the case of the State of Texas versus Clive Kent, on the charge of attempted murder, we the jury find the defendant ... not guilty," the foreman read later that day.

The few spectators gasped and then cheered. Eli must have more than one enemy in that town. The judge dismissed the case, and a wave of relief washed over Kyra. Clive turned to her, grinning from ear to ear, his eyes shining with tears of joy.

"Thank you," he whispered, pulling her into a tight hug.

Kyra hugged him back, a lump in her throat. She knew how much this meant to Clive, but more importantly, how much it meant to Declan. Her whim had paid off, and to see the case end in victory was more than she could have hoped for. It had all happened so fast, but that's how court cases went. And no one, not even the judge, had seemed to want to prosecute. Only Eli's father scowled with furious contempt as the verdict was read.

Kyra turned to Declan, expecting him to share in the jubilation, to hold her in his arms. Instead, he stood apart from the celebration, his expression a stoic mask that betrayed nothing of his thoughts.

"Mr. Kent?" she called softly, approaching him with caution, using his formal name in public. "Are you not delighted?"

His gaze met hers, distant and unreadable. "I am, Miss Bailey. Thank you for your assistance."

The words were polite, almost distant, and they struck her with an ache she hadn't anticipated. She'd believed they'd grown closer over the past few weeks. She'd been certain of it—certain he had meant to kiss her the night before.

She yearned to know what his kisses were like, to feel the warmth of them from her mouth to her toes. The only reason she'd turned away from his kiss was because she couldn't stand to fall for him harder. The trial was over, his mission in Texas done. In a few days he'd go back to Kentucky, where his job and family were. Where his life waited for him.

Perhaps that explained his sudden detachment, his refusal to show even a flicker of vulnerability. He'd retreated behind the same guarded wall that had kept her at arm's length when she first arrived.

Their group filed out of the courthouse, stepping into the humid evening. The earlier rain had done little to ease the sweltering heat, though it brought a faint breeze that offered some relief. As they walked back to the hotel, Clive turned to Kyra, his face flushed with gratitude.

"I'm forever indebted to you, Miss Bailey," he said earnestly, grasping her gloved hand.

Kyra smiled, a warmth blooming in her chest. It was good to be needed, to make a difference. "I'm just glad I could help, Mr. Kent. I know it's taken a huge weight off your brother's shoulders."

Beside her, Declan stiffened, his jaw tightening visibly.

"Are you not pleased?" Kyra asked, nudging him playfully with her shoulder, hoping to draw out some joy.

He didn't return her smile. "I'll be pleased when this is over and I can return to my life, far from all this ... unpleasantness."

With that, he turned and walked ahead, his boots pounding against the damp earth, leaving Kyra with a sudden chill despite the warm air.

"Why is he so angry?" she asked aloud, more to herself than anyone else.

Clive glanced back at her, his easy grin softening. "My brother's never been good at showing his feelings," he said before quickening his pace to catch up with Declan.

But that explanation didn't satisfy her. Declan had come to Texas to free his brother, and now they had succeeded. So why did he seem more troubled than ever? The answer eluded her, but the cold weight of his sudden indifference lingered in her chest.

THE NEXT MORNING, they went to the stables to ready the horses, but they faced a dilemma. There were only two horses between them—Declan's mustang, Blaze, and the gelding Kyra had ridden. Clive had sold his horse to help pay for his trial fees.

"There's only one solution," Clive said, a mischievous twinkle in his eyes. "Miss Bailey must ride with you, brother."

"Absolutely not," Declan said through gritted teeth. He'd barely spoken or looked at Kyra all morning.

"Then she shall ride with me." Clive's smile widened, goading his brother.

"No," Declan practically shouted. "I mean, it wouldn't be proper. She hardly knows you."

"Then shall we leave her behind?" Clive asked, all innocence, but Kyra knew there was nothing innocent in his question.

"Enough," Kyra said, tired of being a pawn in their brotherly games. "Declan, I shall ride with you. Just don't buck me off your horse."

Declan flinched. "Why would you say that?"

"Because you have been looking at me with contempt ever since the trial ended," Kyra accused, placing her hands on her hips.

"You're mistaken," he protested, pushing his white Stetson down on his head.

"I've noticed it too. It may be hotter than a whor—um, well, it may be hot, but you are giving off a bitter chill toward Miss Bailey," Clive said with a chuckle.

Declan scowled at them both but relented, and Kyra climbed onto Blaze, scooting toward the back of the saddle.

Declan swung his leg over the saddle, and Kyra had no choice but to press her body against his back in a snug fit. His skin was warm through his shirt, and a shot of desire blasted through her, along with overwhelming feelings of affection.

"And you are mistaken, Miss Bailey. I won't buck you off my horse," Declan deadpanned. "Only Blaze can do that."

Kyra blinked. Had Declan Kent made a joke?

Declan snapped the reins, sending Blaze into a gallop. Kyra clamped her arms around Declan's midsection, the muscles of his abdomen stiffening under her grasp. Her breasts were pressed against his back, and her heart raced in time with the hoofbeats. She clamped her thighs tightly to Blaze's flanks, overwhelmed by the feel of Declan's body against hers.

Declan concentrated on the path ahead, his back ramrod straight, his hands gripping the reins so tightly that his knuckles turned white. It was like she was a stain that he desperately wanted to be rid of. Her eyes watered with sadness at the thought.

They rode in silence, the only sound the clopping of the horses' hooves on the dusty trail. But as they neared Wylde, Clive spoke up, his voice eager and excited.

"I can't wait to get back to the Bluebonnet," he said, grinning over at Declan and Kyra. "I've got big plans for that place."

Declan's head snapped sideways toward Clive, his eyes blazing. "There are no plans. I have to sell it."

Clive's face fell, confusion and hurt written all over his features. "But why? I've worked so hard for that place."

Declan shook his head, his voice tight. "I've spent every last penny I had on your lawyer, Clive. I haven't worked in a month. I have nothing left. I have to sell the Bluebonnet. Not just for me but for Mama and Isabella."

Clive's eyes widened in shock, and a pang of sympathy for his disappointment hit her.

"You don't have to take care of everyone, Declan," Clive scoffed. "Mama writes to me all the time saying how much she hates the way you smother her, treating her like a child instead of respecting her as your mother."

Declan flinched, his muscles under Kyra's grip tensing. "She said that?"

Clive nodded, his expression hard. "Isabella feels it too. Yes, she's desperate to leave that beast of a husband, but she's riddled with guilt over all the sacrifices you've made for her, forgoing your own happiness. Which I see you're still doing." Clive looked pointedly at Kyra.

"Shut your trap," Declan snapped. "You have no idea what you're talking about."

"I know you, brother," Clive said, a softer tone entering his voice as he trotted next to them. "And it's time for you to live your own life, on your own terms. I realize the irony of saying this now, but I can take care of myself. We all can."

Declan snorted. Kyra understood his disbelief. He had just rescued Clive from a dire fate. But Kyra also admired Clive for forging his own path, away from his family. She knew how hard it was to break free from the expectations and obligations of family.

"Clive is right," Kyra said softly. "You have to start living your life for you. It sounds like this is what your mother and sister desire for you too."

"Like you, Kyra?" he shot back. "You tried to live your life on your own terms, but so far you're still married and held under the thumb of your husband."

Kyra reeled back, the sting of his words punching her at the core of her being.

"I'm under no one's thumb, sir," Kyra said, her voice sharp. "I'm here, aren't I? I've left Henry and I'm ..." She paused, the idea solidifying right there in that moment. "Yes, I'm going to Sioux Falls. It's the only way I can be free of him once and for all. If I go back to Maine, there's no guarantee he'll ever grant me a divorce. He's vengeful and angry. So, yes, this is me living my life on my own terms."

Declan shot a glance over his shoulder, his eyes wide with disbelief, but there was a flicker of hope, perhaps, or longing. But it was gone as quickly as it had appeared, replaced by the same cold, hard mask she knew too well.

"I wish you the best of luck, Kyra," he said stiffly and turned back toward the road, her heart sinking like the *RMS Rhone*. In that moment, it hit her like a shot. She wanted more from Declan than respect and kindness.

She wanted his whole heart, every part of his being.

"You really know how to charm a girl, don't you?" Clive joked, but despite his attempt at humor, the waves of disappointment washed over her like a turbulent sea. Her revelation was not a relief but an unbearable burden.

Blaze stumbled, and Kyra held tighter to Declan's waist, relishing his closeness. Her cheek rested against his back, and she sank into him, wanting to melt into his core and become one. Her chin wobbled and tears seeped out of her eyes, soaking Declan's shirt. She prayed he couldn't feel the dampness.

She was terrified to name what suddenly consumed her.

Unbidden, the four-letter word flashed in her mind, and her stomach churned with nausea. Because if her plan worked and she was granted the divorce, when she returned to Wylde, Declan Kent would be gone.

31

DECLAN

eclan awoke the next morning, his mind reeling from the events of the previous days. They had arrived back at the Bluebonnet Hotel late the night before, exhausted from the long journey and the emotional toll of the trial. He'd barely kept his eyes open as he stumbled to his room, collapsing onto the bed without even bothering to undress.

Now, as he made his way downstairs, he found the hotel and saloon already bustling with activity. Clive was at the center of it all, barking orders and directing the staff with a confident air that Declan had never seen in him before.

"Morning, brother," Clive called out, spotting Declan across the room. "Sleep well?"

"Better than I have in weeks," he admitted.

Clive grinned, clapping Declan on the shoulder. "I still can't believe it," he said, shaking his head in wonder. "I thought for sure I was a goner. But that woman, Miss Bailey, she's something else."

"She certainly is," he agreed, his voice carefully neutral, ignoring the tightness in his chest.

As he watched Clive move through the saloon, chatting with

customers and overseeing the gambling tables, Declan couldn't help but feel a sense of pride. His brother had always been a bit of a wild card, prone to recklessness and impulsivity. But here, in this place, he'd found his calling.

"You're good at this," Declan said, gesturing to the bustling room around them. "Running the Bluebonnet, I mean. It suits you."

Clive looked up, surprise and gratitude flashing in his eyes. "You think so?" he asked, his voice uncharacteristically hesitant. "I haven't always been, but since I was nearly hanged, it's given me a new sense of meaning to my life. I will not waste it."

"It still doesn't mean we won't sell," Declan said firmly. "I need to look at the books, and we need to have some long chats, but this may be your calling after all."

Declan couldn't help but feel conflicted about giving the reins back to Clive. If he listened to his brother, and let go of the responsibilities to his family, then what would be his purpose?

For so long Declan's life had revolved around taking care of his family, being the man of the house and the one everyone turned to in times of need. But now, if Clive continued running the Bluebonnet and his mother and sister led their own lives without his counsel, what would his life be?

He'd go back to his accounting job, which would be exceedingly boring after all his adventures in Wylde. He still bore the financial burden of his mother, and the only way his sister could be free of her husband was if he supported her once she was divorced.

Those facts were unchanged.

"You okay, Declan?" Clive asked, his brow furrowed in concern. "You look a little lost."

Declan shrugged, trying to shake off the melancholy that had settled over him. "Just thinking about the future," he said vaguely. "I'll go check on Scarlett and see how the Belles are faring."

As he made his way back upstairs, his mind churning with

thoughts of an uncertain future, he caught sight of Kyra in the hallway, her satchel in her hand.

"Miss Bailey," he said, his heart lodging in his throat. "You're leaving now?"

She looked up at him, her eyes bright with a mix of excitement and trepidation. "I'm journeying to Sioux Falls," she said, her voice strong and steady. "What I should've done from the start."

"How long will the divorce process take?" he asked, his mind reeling.

"It can take anywhere from a few months to a year, depending on the grounds for divorce," Kyra said, adjusting her satchel. "I'm hoping once Henry sees I'm going through with the divorce no matter what, he won't try to delay it. He's angry now, but when he's home and has Betty in his ear, he may thaw. It's much easier if both parties of the divorce agree to it."

His chest wanted to burst from all the secret yearnings he held tightly inside.

"Safe journeys," he squeezed out, and dashed to his room before he fell apart in front of her.

In his rooms, he pressed his hands against the top of the desk, his shoulders hunched, and sucked down deep breaths, trying to stop the tears that threatened to spill out. Really? Tears? What kind of man was he?

He'd never met a woman like Kyra before, willing to fight for what she wanted, and here he was, blubbering like a baby.

"Declan, what's wrong?" Kyra spoke softly behind him. In his haste, he'd forgotten to shut his door. "Please, after everything, you can confide in me."

"Go away," he grunted.

"I won't," she said, and he almost laughed, because her determination was what he loved most about her. She reached her hand out, caressing his shoulder, and heat shot down his arm.

"I feel untethered," he ground out the words, his fingers gripping the edge of the desk. It wasn't in his nature to be open about his inner thoughts, but he rushed on. "I was resentful when I first arrived and took it out on everyone, especially you. My life had been uneventful, and then I came to this place. Yes, I judged it at first, but I'm changed, and I fear I'll never be the same."

"Do you want to be the same? I'm changed but for the better. Because of this place. Because of you," Kyra said, her voice lowering. "You know, besides the brief attempt with Jacob, you're the only man besides my husband I've touched like that."

Declan spun around. Why would she say that? Didn't she know how badly he wanted her?

"Don't lie to me," he said, angry. "You were with the sheriff."

Kyra smirked. "The sheriff has unique tastes, and all I'll say is his hands were never on me and mine were never on him." Declan frowned, wondering if she were taking him for a fool. "I'm not lying," she insisted. "I won't say anymore because I promised him discretion. Just as I've never told anyone of your ... inexperience."

His cheeks heated at her mention of that.

"Would you like to change that?" she asked, so quietly he wondered if it was a wish whispered inside his head. "Before I go?"

Declan turned slowly, looking upon her face to dissect what game she was playing, because she couldn't really mean—

"I said would you like to change that?" Kyra asked again, dropping her satchel and taking a step closer.

"Don't tease me, Kyra. I won't stand to be made a fool," Declan said, blood already filling his cock at the idea of what she suggested.

"I'm completely serious," she said.

"Why? Why me? Why now?"

She shrugged. "I want to know what it's like to be with another man—a man I trust—before I return here and start this profession in earnest."

"You still want to work as a Belle?" Declan asked, his heart sinking. If she planned to return to that life, any hope of a future together was futile. Her thoughts were not on him.

"It's where my freedom lies," Kyra said. "I have little skill beyond being a wife, and I feel protected here with Scarlett and your brother. It's my best option."

"What of marriage? I mean, once you're divorced, you could marry again. Someone who treats you with respect," Declan said, inching toward his true desire.

"And who shall I marry?" She laughed heartily. "I can't count on a man. I can only count on myself."

Declan's heart crumbled, the hope of ever marrying Kyra drifting away. When he'd first arrived, he would have never have bedded a woman if they weren't married, but he'd be a fool to say no. The only woman he wanted was her, and one taste of love was better than none at all.

"So ..." Kyra glanced up through her lashes, her smile coy with a touch of vulnerability. "Will you have me? We've already done so much. Unless you'd rather I seek out Sheriff Mack."

"No!" he shouted, then cleared his throat. "No. I ... yes. I would like to very much. Since we've already been together in one way, and since I'm leaving."

"Right. Since you're leaving," Kyra said, ducking her head so he couldn't see her eyes.

Declan let out a shaky breath, his fingers tightening around the edge of the desk where he leaned. "Shall we go to the bed or—"

Before he uttered another word, Kyra stepped forward and pressed her lips to his. Declan's mind went blank, his entire being consumed by the feel of her mouth against his. He had never experienced anything like this before—the rush of desire and longing and profound need stole the breath from his lungs.

Her tongue pushed against the line of his lips, and he jolted back. "What was that?" he asked.

"It's called a soul kiss," Kyra said, her bosom pressing against his chest hotly. "Jewell told me about it."

"Oh." Declan swallowed, suddenly unsure how to proceed. There were so many things he didn't know.

"I'm scared too," Kyra said, placing a kiss on the edge of his mouth. "We'll figure it out together."

But Declan wasn't scared. Ignorant, but not scared, and the sound of her ragged breath against his mouth sent every cell in his body into a frenzy. He may not be a professional like the Belles, but he knew how to take control.

In a swift movement, he snatched Kyra's waist and spun her around, pinning her against the desk, pressing his hardness into her soft thigh, more than ready to take this all the way.

"Oh, my," Kyra purred, her hand circling behind his neck, pulling him against the length of her body. "I think I'm going to enjoy this."

KYRA

K yra's heart raced as Declan leaned into the kiss, his fingers tangling in her hair, cradling her head. His tongue flicked out, licking her bottom lip, and she faltered, grasping his shirt to stay upright. Then he nudged her lips apart and slid his tongue inside in a luxurious stroke. A strained moan lodged in her throat, the sensations overwhelming her senses.

Declan tugged Kyra tightly against him, and in a quick movement, he lifted her up, and set her on the desk, his mouth never leaving hers. His tongue swept across hers, and she shoved her hands in his hair, bringing him closer. She trembled in his arms, the kiss almost as good as when she'd pleasured herself. In some ways better because it was Declan touching her, his tongue caressing hers in a fevered dance.

"Oh, Declan," she moaned when his lips moved to her chin. His tongue slid down her neck and over her collarbone. He spent time there, licking across the sensitive skin, trailing kisses down to the tops of her breasts.

"God, you're beautiful," he said, nudging her legs apart, his hands pushing her skirts above her thighs so he could settle against her like a perfect puzzle piece.

Her hands fisted his shirt, trembling slightly. The late afternoon sun filtered through the lace curtains behind them, heating her already scorching skin. Declan glanced up at her as his tongue dipped between her cleavage, her breath catching at the sight of his gaze, his eyes dark with desire and raw devotion that made her pulse skip.

"Are you sure about this, Kyra?" he asked, his voice rough. "Because once we start, I don't know if I can stop. It would take every bit of willpower."

Kyra nodded, her skin flushed with lust. "I want this. I want you."

Declan's gaze bored into hers—seeking one final reassurance before he continued—but how could he not believe her? She wrapped her thighs tightly around him, her tongue hungrily lapping up his kisses.

He made quick work of the buttons on her dress, exposing her corset. His hands yanked it down, seams ripping and buttons flying, clattering to the floor. Her breasts were exposed, spilling out the top of the opened corset, and Declan was transfixed. A shiver of pleasure raced down her spine at his heated look.

His mouth hovered over her right nipple, warm air tickling her skin. One finger traced the underside of her breast, and she arched her back, begging him to take her nipple into his mouth.

"Please," she whimpered, imploring him to put that one tiny part of her body out of its misery.

He did not make her wait long. His lips sucked her pebbled nipple into his mouth, and she shuddered, gasping and mewling as his tongue circled it. Her hands moved down his shirt-clad back, digging her fingers into the hard muscles.

When his mouth released her, the cool air tickled her wet skin, her nipple taut.

"More," she said, pulling him closer.

He obeyed and scooped her other breast into his hand, kneading it. Her head fell back, eyes closed, losing herself in her arousal. He leaned forward and gave that nipple the same care as he did the first. Kyra's hips swayed on the desk as if they had a mind of their own, and her sex pulsed, imagining Declan doing to her most private part what he was doing to her bosom.

Fevered, Kyra grabbed the top of his button-down shirt and tried to yank it apart as he had her bodice, but the buttons didn't budge. Declan lifted his head, and they both laughed at her failure.

"Shall I?" he asked, unbuttoning his shirt swiftly and letting it drop to the floor.

Kyra's mouth watered, her stomach flipping at the sight of this perfect man's physique.

"You're like one of those statues in Rome. Carved to perfection," Kyra said, her breath shallow. Her hands rolled over his firm landscape, her fingers gliding along his well-defined abdomen and skittering atop the waistline of his trousers, his stomach contracting under her caress. A few inches below, there was a conspicuous swell under his trousers.

Her mind faltered, remembering how he'd filled her mouth with what hid beneath the fabric, and Kyra's hand slid down and cupped it, eager to please him.

"Not yet." He snatched her wrist. "Unless you want me to ruin these pants."

"I'd very much like you to ruin me," she said, cocking up one side of her mouth.

All humor left Declan's face, his eyes hooding with lust. He dropped to his knees and shoved her skirts fully above her waist, exposing her womanhood through the large slit in between the legs of her drawers. He let out a guttural sound as he gazed between her legs, and a warm shiver ran down Kyra's back.

"What are you doing?" she asked, scooting back. Surely Declan wouldn't perform that act. She'd seen it during one of her lessons, but Declan wouldn't know of it.

"I'm a very good pupil," he said, glancing up at her, humor in his eyes.

"You had your own lessons?" Kyra blinked, stunned.

"Not exactly, but you see things managing a brothel. I had some questions, and Scarlett filled me in."

Kyra's mouth popped open, and all words left her. Declan—handsome, rugged, selfless Declan—leaned forward, blowing warm air over her sex. Her stomach clenched, and it took everything in her not to slam her legs shut, suddenly shy.

She'd never had a man do this to her. Never even thought of it until she arrived at the Bluebonnet.

The way he stared at her most private place made her want to squirm away. Not because she wasn't desperate to have him pleasure her, but because of how vulnerable it felt.

His tongue flicked out and flattened against her slit, and she fell back, her body screaming out in ecstasy as Declan continued his exploration, worshipping her body with his mouth. Her hips rocked in rhythm with his lips, and a swell of energy rose inside her—a tidal wave of love and longing that threatened to sweep her away along with the crescendo of her release.

Her breath hitched, pulse racing, every nerve on fire as Declan's touch sent shockwaves through her. Her body tightened, curling in on itself, that delicious ache building between her thighs, unbearable yet perfect. She tried to hold on, but he wouldn't let her. His name was on her lips, a desperate whisper.

"Don't hold back," he murmured against her.

"Declan," she gasped, her voice breaking on his name, unable to resist his command.

The world dropped away. Her back arched, mouth open in a silent cry as pleasure surged through her in white-hot waves as he devoured her. It started deep in her core, expanding, consuming her completely. She shattered around him, a tangle of sensation, her body trembling with aftershocks as her release claimed her over and over. Time blurred, leaving nothing but the pulse of her pleasure and the feel of his mouth and tongue.

As she floated back to earth, Declan still kissing her thoroughly, she bit her lip, sadness crashing into her, a startling realization hitting her like a ton of bricks.

Oh, God, she loved him.

The way he made her feel safe and alive all at once, the way his eyes softened when he looked at her, like she was the only thing in the world that mattered.

She loved him. Completely. Fiercely. Desperately.

As fast as this epiphany came, so did the heartbreak, because she knew without a doubt that he didn't feel the same. He couldn't. He was leaving. He had his life in Kentucky, his responsibilities to his mother and sister, far from here, far from her.

She bit her lip, trying to hold back the tears that threatened to spill. It wasn't fair to have her heart snatched by a man who was leaving. She thought she could handle being with him in this way, but now it all felt like a cruel joke, the love she didn't see coming twisting inside her, bittersweet and aching.

Even if he stayed, he'd never see her as anything more than a prostitute, but in that moment, she wanted to give him every part of her, body and soul. In the end, it would leave her hollow and broken—that's why she'd resisted these feelings for so long—but her body screamed to be filled by him, and she wasn't stopping just because her silly heart had fallen for Declan Kent.

33

DECLAN

Declan pressed his lips together, holding back the joy that rained down on him knowing he'd brought Kyra pleasure so thoroughly. She fell back on the desk, panting, her legs loose. Declan kissed her inner thighs, first the left, then the right, before letting her skirts fall back into place.

"I need a moment before the main course." Kyra lifted on her elbows, her voice teasing but strained.

"It may be a quick course," he admitted, his voice raw with lust.

"I don't care as long as it's with you," she said. A hint of sadness tinged her words, but then she smiled and he dismissed it.

With a growl, Declan pulled her to him and kissed her, open-mouthed. Now that he understood the pure delight in tongues sliding together in a forbidden dance, lips sucking and nipping, he never wanted to kiss any other way.

He guided them to the bed, placing her on the edge, standing before her, his hips at her face level. A flicker of doubt crossed her gaze at the sight of his cock pushing against his cotton trousers.

"What is it?" he asked, fearing she'd changed her mind.

"Your member is rather ... large. I worry it'll tear me in two." Kyra glanced up at him, a glimmer of excitement in her eyes.

"We don't have to. If you'd rather—"

"We'll make it work." She cut him off, reaching out toward his cock, but he caught her arm. Declan raised her wrist to his mouth, kissing her palm, a distraction. Kyra moaned softly, gooseflesh covering her skin.

Though he was a virgin, a strange sense of confidence empowered him, as if he understood her inner desires and how to fulfill them. If the new kissing told him anything, it was to trust his instinct. His body knew what to do.

His tongue trailed up her salty-sweet forearm, ending with a kiss on the inside of her elbow. He continued his journey, kissing over her collarbone and down to her ripped corset. He tugged at the ruined material and slid it over her head. Kyra lifted her hips and wiggled out of her skirts until she was left in only her loose drawers, her breasts taut and naked before him.

He licked his tongue across his bottom lip, eager to devour her ripe mounds. His hand cupped the soft skin, warm and ripe, and he leaned forward, sighing when he latched on to her perky nipple.

"Oh my!" Kyra gasped, arching her back to him.

He languidly explored this breast for a second time, leaving no millimeter untouched. When he'd satisfied his craving, he moved on to her other breast. He couldn't leave her unbalanced.

"More," she breathed out, her right hand running down his chest, over his abdomen, and then down the front of his pants. The thin fabric of his trousers blocked her from touching him fully, but it didn't stop the drop of liquid from escaping his tip, darkening the fabric.

He jerked his hips backward and his mouth popped off her nipple. "You're playing with fire, darling."

"I like the heat." She fluttered her lashes, the picture of mock innocence.

He traced the outside of her thigh with his free hand until he reached the top of her drawers, pulling at the string that held them on her waist. She lifted her hips and shimmied out of the garment, all the while Declan's mouth never left her breast.

Her legs spread and he sank against her, his hardness pressing against her naked sex, hot and welcoming. Desire rushed through his veins, his cock screaming for its own pleasure to be sated.

"I can't take it," she moaned. "If you don't make love to me this instant, I shall take care of it myself."

To prove her point, she dipped her hand between their bodies, but Declan would have none of that. He snatched her arm and pinned it behind her back. Her eyes lit with excitement.

"You want me," he said. It wasn't a question, and his heart raced with delight hearing her mewl and moan when he touched her. "I want you too, but not until you're clawing at my back, so close to climax you'll go mad without your release. That's when I shall enter you."

Her lips parted, so pretty and pink, her mouth a perfect O. He circled the inside of her thighs with his thumb, inching toward the part of her he'd feasted on earlier. He tilted his head toward her face, then slid his tongue along her jawline and whispered in her ear. "Are you ready for more?"

A blush ran up her neck, a low moan her only verbal response. If it had been any other woman, he'd push into her that moment. It was nearly impossible to be restrained when his cock was a solid rod, aching to feel the sweet insides of Miss Kyra Bailey. But this would be his only time with her, and he wanted to savor every moment.

Declan raked his gaze over her naked form. Kyra was so beautifully erotic, perched on the bed, spread open. He had to look away, sucking down several deep breaths, nearly losing it. She hadn't even touched him and he'd nearly spilt his seed. That's what this woman did to him.

"Enough of this nonsense." Kyra gripped his biceps and dragged him on top of her, lying back on the bed. "Put us out of our misery."

He stilled above her, his eyes locking with hers. She stared back with an intensity that made his heart ache. For a long moment, they said nothing, the words *I love you* hovering on the tip of his tongue, but he kept that thought hidden.

Declan shed his trousers and underclothes and then hovered above her. Kyra's eyes were locked on his cock pointing toward her seductive center. Was that fear that crossed her face? He tilted his hips away and she flung her gaze up.

"We don't have to—"

"Don't you dare back out on me now, Declan Kent." Her fingers dug into his hips and he sank down, his tip parting her folds.

His cock pulsed, so ready. He nudged forward, his intent to go gently, but she was so slick, so ready for him, his tip slid in quickly, her soft flesh swallowing his girth.

"Oh God!" he cried out, his muscles clenching, trying to resist going over the edge.

For years he'd wondered what it would be like to be inside a woman. In the privacy of his own room, he'd touched himself, imagining what a woman would feel like around his cock, and so far, the reality had blown away all expectations.

"I'm so close," Kyra whispered in his ear, her hands pressing into his backside, shoving him further into her depths. "Don't hold back."

Declan rocked his hips, moving inside her as a new urgency, more desperate and glorious than before, took hold, building. The feel of her muscles clasping his cock put his hand to shame. There was nothing like the warmth of her, the tightness of her womanhood, the sounds of her arousal.

Heat surged through every part of him. Declan's breath stuttered as he gazed down at her—his Kyra—her skin slick with sweat, her body arching beneath him, clutching him tighter with every roll of her hips. He couldn't believe this was happening. He couldn't believe *she* was happening. He'd thought of this moment a hundred times, but nothing had prepared him for how she felt, how they fit together. Her fingers dug into him, nails biting into his skin, pulling him closer, keeping him anchored to her.

His heart pounded harder with every thrust, driving him faster toward the edge, but all he could think about was her—her eyes fluttering closed, her lips parted with soft gasps, the way she whispered his name like he was the only man who had ever mattered. Maybe he was. Maybe this moment was more than a fleeting indulgence for her. Maybe it was something real.

But how could it be? She wanted her independence, not another man to hold her back. She couldn't possibly love him. Could she? The doubt gnawed at Declan, even now, even as the wave rose inside him, the pleasure coiling tight, desperate to break free.

Declan's throat tightened. He wanted to tell her. He wanted to say the words he'd been holding back for so long, but his body was on fire, every nerve alight with a need so strong it swallowed everything else. He was losing control. He could feel it. He was close, so close.

"Kyra," Declan gasped, her name torn from his lips as his hips pumped, the heat spiraling through him in a way that left him trembling. His muscles tensed, the pressure inside him threatening to break. Declan couldn't stop it. God, he didn't want to stop it.

Kyra's eyes opened, locking on to his, and in that moment, he was lost. Completely, utterly lost. And then he shattered.

He roared, his release surging through him, every ounce of restraint vanishing, his body shaking with the force of it. They moved as one, frantic and primal, until Kyra cried out, shuddering and trembling as they reached the peak together.

Declan collapsed against her, burying his face in the crook of her neck, breathless and undone. It was more than making love. More than their bodies being joined as one. Their souls had intertwined in a perfect union.

~

AFTERWARD, they lay tangled on the sweat-dampened sheets, their breathing gradually slowing. Kyra rested her head on Declan's chest, her fingers tracing idle patterns on his skin.

"That was perfect." She lifted onto her elbow, her voice tinged with an ache. "You are a wonderful lover, Declan Kent." She looked away, her voice barely above a whisper. "One day you'll make a woman very happy."

Declan's heart contracted painfully. She was the only woman he wanted. But he couldn't say that. He'd never hold her back from her true desires, but he couldn't stay there and pretend.

"I'm not big on goodbyes," he said gruffly, sitting up and moving away from her, from any hope of her being his completely.

When she didn't respond, he glanced over his shoulder. Kyra's face was covered in hurt and confusion, and a pang of regret hit him like a jab in the ribs.

"I suppose you'll be gone when I come back," Kyra said, swinging her legs to the other side of the bed and pulling her drawers to her waist, covering the part of her Declan would be dreaming about for the rest of his life.

"My life is in Kentucky." He paused, the ache in his chest

clawing at his heart. The Bluebonnet had grown on him. Kyra wasn't the only thing he'd miss when he was gone.

Declan yanked his trousers on and then walked around to Kyra, pressing a kiss to her temple before releasing her. "You're a woman to be reckoned with, Kyra Bailey. My world has changed because of you."

Kyra laughed, but it sounded hollow. "For bad or good?"

"Definitely for good." Declan gently placed her clothing next to her.

In the adjoining room, he sat behind his desk and waited as she dressed. He wasn't sure how one acted after being with a woman you would never see again.

Dressed, Kyra walked into the room, smiling at Declan, who sat stoically behind his desk, his heart sinking, the hope of love slipping away.

"You look very much like the stern boss you were when you first arrived." Kyra smiled. She reached out and placed her hand on top of his. "You're a good man, Declan. No matter what happens, I want you to remember that."

He could have sworn there was a glimmer of tears in her eyes. "And you're a good woman, Kyra," he said, pulling his hand from hers.

"Perhaps, we'll meet again," Kyra said, her face shuttering. "Goodbye, Mr. Kent."

Declan forced a smile. "Safe travels, Miss Bailey."

34

DECLAN

Declan handed Blaze over to the stable hand and wiped the sweat from his brow. Kyra had been gone less than twelve hours, but every minute felt like a lifetime. He'd barely slept, the smell of her lingering on his bedding, the images imprinted on his mind.

In the morning, he'd ripped the quilt from his legs and went straight to the stables, took Blaze out, and rode the mustang hard. The morning air was sweltering, but he barely noticed it, his entire being numb with the pain of her absence.

He had known this moment was coming, but nothing could have readied him for the feeling of loss that consumed him. The next few days passed in a blur of anger and frustration, with Declan snapping at everyone who crossed his path. He knew he was being unfair, that his foul mood was affecting the entire hotel. But he couldn't help himself, his despair manifesting as a sharp-edged irritability that drove everyone away. Even Clive, who'd always been able to coax a smile or a laugh out of him, no matter how dire the circumstances, had found himself on the receiving end of Declan's wrath.

Declan was yelling at a customer in the saloon, for some

reason he couldn't remember, and Clive leapt from his perch at the bar, stomping over to him.

"Damn it, Declan," he exploded, slamming his hand down on a table in frustration. "Go lock yourself in your room. You're bad for business."

Declan glared furiously at his brother.

"Or go back to Kentucky. I saw the telegram from the bank. They'll fire you if you don't return soon." Clive exhaled, giving up the fight. "We all know why you're miserable. If you're not going home, then stop being such a jerk and go after her."

Declan's jaw clenched so tightly he could feel his teeth grinding together. "It's too late. She's gone, and there's nothing I can do about it," he growled.

Clive shook his head, a sad smile playing at the corners of his mouth. "It's never too late, brother," he said, his tone uncharacteristically gentle. "Look at me. I've been given a second chance. Thanks to you. And to Miss Bailey."

Declan turned away, his eyes stinging. Clive was right. He should be on the next train chasing after the woman who held his heart. But a fear of rejection and further heartbreak held him back.

"I have a proposition for you," Clive said, breaking the tense silence. "I'm no good with money and numbers, you know that. And I've got a mighty temper. But I'm calmer when you're here. And you know how to run a business."

Declan's head snapped up, his eyes widening in surprise. "What are you saying?"

"Be my partner." Clive nodded, his grin widening. "I've already written to Mama asking her to come down and join us. And I think I can convince Isabella to come with her, and we can finally figure out how to get her out of that god-awful marriage."

A flicker of hope sparked to life in his chest, a glimmer of possibility that he hadn't dared to entertain before. Maybe he could find a way to build a life here.

"Alright," he said, his voice rough with emotion. "I'll write to Mama and Izzy and confirm this is what they want. If they really are up for the adventure, I'll find a house for them here, then travel up to get them. We'll need to go over the books and find money because my savings are wiped out. And we'll set up a plan for you to pay me back. Agreed?"

Clive's grin widened, and he reached out to clasp Declan's hand in a firm shake. "Agreed," he said, his eyes sparkling with excitement. "Don't you go repeating this, but I've felt lost without my family here. It'll be grounding to have everyone together. A new start."

THE NEXT TWO weeks passed in a whirlwind of activity, with Declan throwing himself into the day-to-day operations of the Bluebonnet, searching for a house, and securing a loan against the business. He pored over the account books, streamlining expenses and maximizing profits, until the hotel and saloon were running more smoothly than ever before. He was also looking into side ventures to scale profits.

He enjoyed the work, the sense of purpose and accomplishment that came with building something tangible, something that he owned. But even as he threw himself into his new role, he couldn't quite shake the nagging feeling that his life was incomplete.

He was in the office going over the latest batch of invoices when a knock at the door startled him from his thoughts.

"Come in," he called out, expecting Scarlett. He'd officially put her in charge of the brothel, which she managed as proficiently as she had when Declan had first arrived. Of all the businesses, the brothel had always been the most efficiently run. Of course, it was not officially a business but, with a few tweaks, they could file taxes legally and not fear the authorities shutting them down.

Especially since many of the authorities frequented the saloon for the company of the ladies.

The door swung open, and Declan's jaw dropped in shock as a familiar figure stepped into the room.

"Hello, big brother," the auburn-haired woman said, a teasing smile playing at the corners of her mouth. "Long time no see."

"Izzy?" Declan whispered, rising slowly to his feet. "But how? I was coming up next week to fetch you."

His sister beamed, her green eyes sparkling. He hadn't seen her this vibrant in a long time.

"Billy started getting suspicious, so Mama and I changed our tickets and here we are. Don't worry, I'm fine," she confirmed, her voice trembling slightly. "I don't think Billy will come looking for me. He's too lazy."

A wave of gratitude washed over him, and he crossed the room in two long strides, gathering his sister into his arms and holding her tight.

"I've missed you so much," he murmured into her hair, his own eyes stinging with tears. "And I'm so sorry, Iz. Sorry for not being there when you needed me, for getting you trapped in that awful marriage."

Isabella pulled back slightly, her hands coming up to cup Declan's face in her palms. "You have nothing to apologize for," she said firmly, her gaze unwavering. "You didn't know he was a monster when you agreed to the marriage. I loved him. You did the best you could, Deck. And now, thanks to you, I have a chance to start over, to build a new life for myself."

"Where's Mama?" Declan glanced over his sister's shoulder, expecting her to come barreling in with the stories of their travels across the country.

"Giving Clive an earful about ending up in jail. She's not really angry. He just gave her a scare."

Declan's heart swelled, knowing his family was together again.

"We're going to get you that divorce," he promised, his voice rough. "And I've found a house for us, a home."

Isabella's smile widened, and she hugged him again, her slender frame shaking with a mixture of laughter and tears.

As they made their way downstairs, arm in arm, Declan's heart leapt at the sight of his mother talking to Clive in the lobby.

"My boys," she said, her voice trembling as she gathered them both into her arms. "Let us never be apart again."

Declan hugged her back, his heart full to bursting. But even as he basked in the warmth of their presence—his family, here in Wylde!—a flicker of sorrow tapped at his heart.

Kyra had made it to Sioux Falls and her gamble had paid off. As soon as Henry realized she wasn't returning to Maine and that she planned to seek a divorce with or without him, he caved and agreed not to fight it. It would still be months before it was finalized, but the process toward her freedom had begun. Kyra hadn't written to Declan personally, but Scarlett fed him nuggets of information from her correspondence with her niece. Declan had hoped Kyra would write to him, but after all these weeks, there'd been nothing.

Kyra said she'd return to the Bluebonnet after the divorce, but if she did indeed return, it would be a blessing and a curse. How would Declan survive day after day having her so close, but never truly having her?

KYRA

Three months later

Kyra stepped off the train, her heart pounding with a mixture of excitement and trepidation. The bustling platform of Wylde, Texas, was just as she remembered it, the air thick with the scent of coal smoke and the shouts of the porters as they loaded and unloaded luggage.

But even as she looked around, drinking in the familiar sights and sounds, she couldn't shake the feeling of unease that had settled in the pit of her stomach.

It was late September, and the unrelenting heat of summer was gone, replaced by the crisp autumn air and changing leaves. Scarlett had been in correspondence during Kyra's entire stay in Sioux Falls, keeping her up-to-date on the happenings at the Bluebonnet. The most surprising piece of information had been that Declan had not left, but chosen to stay and partner with his brother.

Kyra had been eager for more information on Declan, but Scarlett didn't mention him unless it related to the brothel.

For a brief moment, Kyra let herself dream of a life with

Declan. She wondered if he had found someone by now. He was a good-looking, eligible bachelor. It wouldn't take long for him to be snatched up.

She couldn't bear to think of him with another woman, but that's what men like Declan did—they went on with their lives and found the perfect wife to make a perfect family. Children included, which she could never give him even if they were together.

As she made her way down the dusty main street, her satchel clutched tightly in her hand, she caught sight of his familiar figure standing outside the doors to the saloon.

Declan Kent.

Her heart leapt into her throat. He was even more handsome than she remembered—strong and bookish with his glasses, his broad chest, and tanned skin. She blushed thinking of the last time they were together. Excitement swelled in her chest, and she quickened her pace.

As she drew closer, a beautiful young woman with fiery auburn hair and sparkling eyes stepped out of the saloon and rested her hand lightly on his arm. Declan's face lit up, and he leaned in and said something to her, and the young woman laughed heartily.

The ground dropped out from beneath her feet. Kyra had known that Declan might have moved on, that he might have found someone else in the time she'd been gone. But it didn't stop the knife from twisting in her heart.

A carriage came barreling down the road, and Kyra yelped, jumping out of its way toward the hotel. Declan's head snapped up, his eyes widening in shock as he caught sight of her. For a long moment, they simply stared at each other, the world around Kyra fading away.

"Miss Bailey?" Declan said, his voice low and fervent. "Is it really you?"

She nodded, her throat too tight to speak. She wanted to

run to him, to throw herself into his arms and never let go. But the presence of the other woman held her back, a painful reminder of all that had changed in the months she'd been away.

"What are you doing here?" Declan asked, taking a tentative step towards her. "I thought you were still in Sioux Falls."

Kyra swallowed hard, forcing herself to meet his gaze. "I've accomplished what I went to do," she said, her voice barely above a whisper, glancing at the woman beside him. "I said I'd come back to the Bluebonnet. So here I am. I didn't realize how much I missed this place until this moment. I suppose I even missed you, too, Mr. Kent."

She laughed, trying to cover the truth in her words. A flash of hope and longing flickered in Declan's eyes, but his gaze darted to the woman beside him, and his expression shuttered, becoming unreadable once more.

"I see," he said, his tone carefully neutral. "Well, welcome back, Miss Bailey. I suppose you'll be seeking out your aunt to discuss your employment."

A flare of anger lit inside her chest at his formalness, at the way he held himself apart from her. It was irrational. She had no right to expect anything from him but cordiality. But the sight of him with another woman, looking so comfortable and happy, nearly killed her.

"Actually, Mr. Kent," she said, swallowing over the ache, "I've had a lot of time to ponder my future, and I've decided not to go back to work with my aunt. I'm grateful for that experience, but I feel there may be other ways I can share my talents. Ways that you'd certainly find more respectable." The last sentence dripped with sarcasm.

Declan's brow furrowed in confusion. She crossed her arms over her chest, a perverse satisfaction at having thrown him off-balance. She knew she was being childish, that she was falling back into their old pattern of sniping at each other. But it was better than letting him see how much he'd hurt her, even if it was unintentional.

"I had a lot of knowledge to offer the women in Sioux Falls, and I realized there may be other women like them. Women who lacked the knowledge I had gained over the years. After much back-and-forth with my aunt, I've decided to open a special type of school for them," she said, lifting her chin proudly. "To give them the education and opportunities that I never had. And to arm them with knowledge of the law and how it can work for and against them."

Declan's eyes widened in surprise, and for a moment, Kyra thought she saw a flicker of admiration in their depths. But then his gaze shuttered once more, and he nodded stiffly, his expression unreadable.

"That's a noble idea, Miss Bailey," he said, his tone carefully polite. "I wish you all the best in your endeavors."

Kyra's temper flared, and before she could stop herself, she spoke, her voice sharp and cutting. "You wish me all the best? Really, Dec—Mr. Kent? Spare me your platitudes. I thought we were friends."

Next to him, the young woman's green eyes flashed with interest, but there was no anger or jealousy in her gaze, only keen curiosity.

Declan's jaw clenched, and for a moment, Kyra thought he might snap back at her, might give in to the old familiar pattern of their arguments. But then he took a deep breath and stepped forward.

"Miss Bailey," he said, his voice placating, "why are you so angry with me?"

She shook her head, her eyes stinging. "I'm not," she said, her voice trembling slightly.

Declan had moved on, and Kyra must find a way to be happy for him. She'd already shown too much. What if he guessed the truth? That she wasn't angry, she was heartbroken.

She put out her hand and plastered on a large smile for the young woman at his side. "I'm Miss Kyra Bailey. I'm pleased to see Mr. Kent has found such a lovely woman. I'm pleased for you both."

But she wasn't pleased, not even close. The thought of him building a life and a future that didn't include her gutted her to the core.

"Kyra, what are you talking about?" Declan asked, his frown deepening.

She gestured towards the woman. "I assume you two are courting? Or perhaps you are already engaged. If so, then—"

Declan's eyes widened, and then, to Kyra's shock, he threw back his head and laughed.

"That's why you're upset?" he said, shaking his head in disbelief. "Because you believe *we* are engaged?"

"I—" Kyra's cheeks flamed. Why was he laughing at her discomfort? Had he guessed that it was she who desperately wanted to be on his arm, to be his wife? That it was all she'd thought about for the past three months? That it consumed her every waking moment?

She shook her head and hurried into the saloon, humiliation wrapping around her. She had to escape before she broke.

"Kyra," Declan said, following her inside.

It was dark, and it took Kyra's eyes a moment to adjust to the dim lighting.

"Are you okay?"

Kyra's chin wobbled at the question, and she turned on him. Everything she'd been holding in since she left him in his room came tumbling out, too much to hold in any longer.

"No, I'm not okay!" she cried, tears spilling out of her eyes. "I'm a wreck. I thought I'd be okay coming back here. Why do you have to be here? Why couldn't you have gone back to Kentucky as you'd said? Maybe then, maybe I wouldn't be such a... maybe I could finally..."

Her voice cracked, and she bent over, sobs wracking her body.

"What I want isn't in Kentucky," Declan said, looking utterly miffed by her outburst.

Kyra's sobs turned into a wail, and she clamped her hand over her mouth. He must have met that woman right after she left. That's why he stayed. In the back recesses of her mind, after Scarlett wrote her, she'd thought maybe Declan had stayed for her, but he'd stayed for someone else.

Now that the dam had burst, she couldn't stop crying. In a haze, she felt Declan guiding her up the stairs, away from the prying eyes of the employees and patrons.

When she opened her eyes, she stood in Declan's room. The desk, the bed, everything was a reminder of what she could never have, and she fell apart all over again.

"Miss Kyra Bailey," Declan demanded behind her. "Are you in love with me?"

DECLAN

Kyra loved him. She must. Understanding had struck Declan like a lightning bolt. It was the only explanation for her sudden distress at what she assumed was his engagement. Even if it was a false assumption. Oh, he might be kidding himself, letting himself hope like that, but the evidence seemed clear.

"Kyra," Declan said again, his voice barely above a whisper. After months of pining for her, he had to know. "Do you love me?"

Her shoulders shook, her head bent away from him, unable or unwilling to speak through her sobs. She wasn't denying it.

Declan's heart leapt for joy, but his head wasn't ready to fully believe it yet. Asking her outright was only upsetting her more. Perhaps if he brought them back on familiar footing, he could ease her distress.

"It's not very ladylike to cry over an engaged man," he teased.

Kyra's eyes flashed with anguish, her tears momentarily forgotten. "How can you jest while I'm obviously suffering? It's cruel, Declan. I thought we were friends, at least."

Her gray eyes glimmered with her tears, her cheeks pink from her distress, her lips parted. Declan smiled. It had been too long since he'd looked upon her face, and it took the breath from his lungs. Unable to resist, Declan pulled Kyra against his chest.

She yelped, her eyes wide with surprise, but before she could protest, he pressed his lips to hers in a searing kiss. For a moment, Kyra melted against him, her hands clutching at his shirt. But then, as if remembering herself, she pushed him away, shock written across her face.

"You're engaged!" she gasped, her voice a mixture of outrage and disbelief.

Declan shrugged, his eyes twinkling with barely suppressed mirth. "We've crossed forbidden lines before, haven't we? You were married when we were together."

Kyra's eyes widened, and she stepped back, her hand covering her mouth. Declan was about to tell her the truth when the door swung open, and Isabella walked in.

"Oh! I'm sorry," Isabella said when she saw them.

"What have I done?" Kyra's face drained of color, horror wrapping around her. "I'm so sorry."

Declan opened his mouth to put Kyra out of her misery, but his sister spoke first.

"Declan, you scoundrel. Bringing a woman up here," Isabella began, but then her expression changed as understanding dawned and she clapped giddily. "Wait? Is this the young lady you've been pining over? Miss Bailey?"

"Pining? Why would you say that to your fiancée?" Kyra's gaze darted between Declan and Isabella.

"Fiancée?!" Isabella chortled loudly. "Oh, no, Miss Bailey. I'm his sister. Isabella."

"Your sister?" Understanding dawned on Kyra's face and she whipped her head around to Declan. "And you said nothing, teasing me?"

Declan shrugged, a wicked smile spreading across his face.

"I'll leave you to get caught up," Isabella said with a knowing smile. "We'll speak properly later."

As soon as the door clicked shut, Kyra spun on Declan, fury in her eyes.

"You were playing me? How could you?" Her fists hit his chest and he grabbed them, yanking her into an embrace.

Kyra's body tensed in his arms, but Declan's fingers traced the curve of her hips and her muscles eased. He dipped his head down, lowering his lips until they ghosted her mouth, close but not touching.

"Say the words, Kyra. Put me out of my misery."

Her breath came in short gasps, Declan could see the desire and frustration warring within her, the way she fought against the words that threatened to spill out.

"Say it," he demanded.

She tried to wiggle out of his grasp, but Declan held fast, his hands like steel bands.

"Fine!" she cried out furiously. "I love you. Are you satisfied?"

"No," he whispered in her ear. "I'm very much unsatisfied." He nudged her with his hips, his hardened cock pressing against her pelvis.

"Is that all you want from me?" Kyra said, her face falling.

"Not *all*," he said, his lips brushing across her ear. "I want your body, but I also want your heart." He leaned back on his heels, his eyes capturing hers. "You've had mine for months."

"What are you saying?" Kyra asked, blinking in disbelief.

"I love you, Kyra Bailey. I've been a miserable sod since you left. All I've ever wanted is you. Body, heart, and soul."

Kyra shook her head, confusion on her face. "But not as your wife. As a mistress, right? A principled man like you wouldn't want me. Not after everything I've done here."

Declan cupped her face again, forcing her to meet his gaze. "I don't care about that. You're all I want, Kyra. All I need. Don't you understand? You've turned my world upside down, and I never want it to be right-side up again. Of course I want you to be my wife."

A little sound squeaked out of Kyra, and Declan sealed his lips with hers. A dam broke, and all the feelings they'd been holding back came rushing out in a fevered torrent. Declan's hands tangled in Kyra's hair, while hers clutched at his shoulders, pulling him closer. Months of longing and misunderstanding poured out between them.

When Kyra finally pulled away, there were tears in her eyes.

"Declan, we can't marry," she whispered, her voice trembling. "I'm barren. You deserve so much more than I can offer."

He shook his head, and his eyes filled with his own tears, aching to take away her pain. "I have all the family I need, Kyra. My brother, my sister, my mother, and you. Don't you see? My life was empty before you came into it. Now, it's full to bursting."

Kyra searched his face, then let out a shaky breath. "Are you sure? Truly sure? Because I couldn't bear it if you changed your mind later."

"I've never been more sure of anything in my life," he murmured against her lips as his fingers worked at the buttons of Kyra's dress, eager to feel skin against skin.

"Oh, Declan." In a rush, Kyra tugged his shirt off and rid him of his trousers until their discarded clothing was piled at their feet, Kyra left in her thin chemise and Declan in his loose undergarment.

Declan trailed kisses down the column of Kyra's neck, reveling in the way she arched against him. Her nails scraped lightly down his back, drawing a low groan from deep in his chest.

They explored each other slowly, savoring every curve, every valley, making up for lost time. The rest of the world fell away.

There was no brothel, no complicated past, no uncertain future. There was only this moment, this connection, this love that had grown between them against all reason.

"You're beautiful," Declan whispered, tugging the top of the chemise off her shoulders until it fell to her waist. His lips skimmed the tops of her breasts, basking in the fact that he was allowed to touch her again.

He looked up at Kyra, a thrill running down his spine as she watched him with open desire.

"I love how your nipples tighten when you're aroused," Declan said, his voice hoarse with the admission.

He rolled her nipple between his fingers, and she moaned, arching her back toward him. He scooped her breast into his right hand and gently nibbled the pebbled apex, then clamped his lips over it, sucking it into his mouth.

"Oh, Declan," she sighed, her hands tightening around his shoulders.

Her shortness of breath and the rapid beating of her heart filled him with power. He loved knowing he could do this to her, fill her with this urgency. He licked his way across the valley between her breasts, then took her other nipple into his mouth, rolling his tongue around the taut tip.

Not one to wait for what she wanted, Kyra moved her hands down his chest, over his pectorals, and pinched his nipples in union.

He gasped, red-hot desire rushing to the core of his body.

"I can play rough too." She smiled coyly. She continued her assault, running her nails down his abdomen and gripping the top of his undergarment.

In a flash, she tugged at the string that held them up, and they fell to the floor, exposing his erect manhood. For a moment, Kyra said nothing, didn't move, only stared at him. Declan squirmed under her scrutiny, his cock hardening further, the small veins popping along the shaft.

"Oh," she said, her jaw dropping. "It twitched."

Declan couldn't take much more of this. Could a man climax from just a look?

"Enough," Declan finally said, yanking her chemise down until it pooled at her feet. "I want you to be mine."

Kyra locked her gaze on his. "Not if I make you mine first."

KYRA

Kyra's heart pounded rapidly as Declan gazed intently at her most intimate part. Heat shot into her sex, her muscles pulsing, anticipating what was to come. She'd fantasized about this for months, but now that the moment was here, it was more intoxicating than she could have imagined.

"I've waited too long, dreaming of your body, dreaming of the feel of you around my manhood," Declan said, as if reading her mind. "You are marvelous, Kyra."

"That's exactly how I feel," she murmured.

"You also think you're marvelous?" Declan teased.

Kyra burrowed her head in his shoulder, giggling as warmth flooded through her. "No. You're marvelous, too."

Declan's strong hands lifted her effortlessly, and she wrapped her legs around his waist as he carried her to the bed. When he laid her down on the soft quilt, a thrill ran through her. In a swift movement, she flipped onto her hands and knees, her backside facing him, her body burning for him.

"What are you doing?" Declan asked, his voice a mix of surprise and raw desire.

A wicked smile played on her lips as she glanced over her

shoulder. "Married women talk," she said softly, her voice teasing. "And they had a lot to say about matters of the marriage bed." She watched his reaction, enjoying the way his eyes darkened with lust. "This positioning was suggested, and it sounded delectable."

She could see the struggle in Declan's expression as he tried to hold back. This was what she loved about him—how he could be so tender and yet so passionate, all at once.

"It's like ..." Declan's gaze traveled between her legs, her sex open and ready for the taking. "Like an animal."

"Primal, yes," she whispered, feeling the heat of his eyes boring into her backside. "I was told that if you wrap your hand around my hip and touch me here"—she touched her clit, demonstrating— "while in the act, it will send me into a frenzy."

The sound of his moan sent a shiver down her spine. She could feel his need for her, which only heightened her own. She wanted him to lose control, to give in to the primal urges.

"Scoot toward me," Declan demanded, his voice thick with heat.

Kyra did as he commanded, her body responding instinctively to his voice. When her ankles hung off the edge of the bed, he wrapped his hands around her hips, his touch firm and possessive. Her breath hitched as he positioned himself behind her, the tip of his manhood nudging her entrance, and her entire body trembled with anticipation.

He slowly slid inside her, inch by agonizing inch. Kyra gasped, the sensation both torturous and exquisite. She was filled with him to the hilt, every nerve in her body alive with pleasure.

As instructed, his hand slid around her hip, his fingers rubbing her sensitive nub. She cried out, the pleasure of his hands on her, his manhood filling her sex, nearly overwhelming.

"Yes, Declan," she moaned, unable to hold back the flood of sensation that coursed through her.

His fingers worked her with skillful precision, sending waves of pleasure zipping through her. Her hips rocked back and forth of their own accord, chasing the release she so desperately needed. The friction, the heat, the fullness of him—it was all too much and yet not enough. She wanted more, needed more.

Little beads of sweat formed on her back, and when Declan leaned forward to lick them away, the sensation sent her spiraling closer to the brink. Her body was a live wire, every touch igniting sparks of pleasure that threatened to consume her.

The rhythm of their bodies quickened into a frantic pace. The gentleness from earlier was gone, replaced by a raw need that left them both breathless. Declan's hips thrust against her backside, pumping in unison, as the tension built within her, coiling tighter and tighter until it snapped.

Kyra cried out his name, her muscles convulsing around him, as she was hit with the force of her climax. The pleasure was so intense, so all-consuming, that for a moment she floated above her own body.

As she writhed on her knees, a roar ripped out from behind her. Declan's body trembled from his release, intensifying Kyra's already cosmic climax.

When their bodies went slack, spent from their lovemaking, Declan wrapped his arms around her waist, his breath hot against her skin.

"I love you," Declan sighed, his voice catching. "I love you so damn much."

Kyra's heart swelled with happiness. She flipped onto her back and pulled him on top of her, needing to feel his warmth, his closeness.

"Don't forget ..." she teased before she kissed him deeply. "I said it first."

～

Hours later, they lay with their limbs intertwined, their bodies spent from an afternoon of lovemaking. But even now, Kyra didn't want to leave his embrace. She was safe here, cherished, and more loved than she'd ever been in her life.

She lifted her head and looked at him, mischief dancing in her eyes. "You know," she said, tracing idle patterns on his chest, "I'm not sure one man is enough for me. Perhaps I should send a note to Sheriff Mack—"

Before she could finish, Declan growled playfully and rolled them over, pinning her beneath him. The look in his eyes sent a thrill of excitement through her.

"Is that so, *Mrs. Kent?*" he asked, his voice low and husky. "I think I might need to remind you just how satisfying one man can be."

Kyra's laughter turned into a gasp as Declan's fingers found that sensitive spot below her belly button. The sensation sent shockwaves of pleasure through her, making her body arch beneath him.

"Mrs. Kent?" she managed to ask, breathless. "Aren't you getting a bit ahead of yourself?"

Declan pulled back, his expression suddenly serious. "Say you'll marry me, Kyra," he said, his voice filled with conviction.

Her heart skipped a beat, and tears pricked at the corners of her eyes.

"Yes," she whispered, pulling him in for another kiss. "Yes, of course I'll marry you, Declan."

The sun cast beams of light across their skin, but nothing could match the warm glow inside her. A sense of peace settled over Kyra. She'd never expected to find a man like this.

"I love you," Declan murmured, kissing her forehead.

"I love you too," she replied, snuggling closer to him, her heart full to bursting. "Always."

As Declan shifted beside her, his member rubbed against her

thigh. "I hope you're ready for a lifetime of this," Declan said, his smile wicked.

"I hope you're prepared for a lifetime of sass and stubbornness," Kyra retorted, winking at him.

Declan pulled her closer, his expression intense. "It's all I've ever wanted, because it's all you."

Kyra marveled at how much had changed since they'd first met. She had come to Wylde looking for an escape, but instead, she had found something far more precious. True love with Declan, a family in her aunt and the Bluebonnet Belles, a purpose in helping other women like herself, and an independence she never dreamt she could have with a man by her side.

"I don't ever want to leave this room," Kyra said, stretching her body along the length of him.

Declan smoothed her hair behind her shoulder and kissed down her neck, over her décolletage, and then wrapped his lips around her nipple, sucking it into his mouth.

She moaned, arching into him.

Declan popped his lips off momentarily and looked up at her through his thick lashes. "That can be arranged."

Kyra giggled, thoroughly satisfied.

All she needed was right here.

EPILOGUE

Kyra

Kyra stood on her tiptoes, reaching to hang a wreath of pine boughs and holly berries above the Bluebonnet Hotel's main entrance. The crisp December air nipped at her cheeks, but her heart was warm with the joy of the season.

"A little to the left, Kyra," Isabella called from below, using her keen eye for detail.

Kyra adjusted the wreath, securing it with a red ribbon. "How's that?" she asked, stepping back to admire their handiwork.

The hotel lobby was transformed into a festive wonderland. Garlands of evergreen draped the banisters, their rich scent filling the air. Candles flickered in every window, casting a warm glow over the room. In the corner stood a modest pine tree adorned with strings of popcorn, paper chains, and small, carved wooden ornaments.

Mei approached, her arms full of colorful paper lanterns. Kyra had suggested everyone decorate with items from their various cultures to add some variety and a personal touch to the holiday season.

"In China, we celebrate the Dongzhi Festival near this time," Mei explained, hanging the lanterns carefully. "It's about family reunion and hope for the coming year."

Maeve chimed in, her Irish lilt adding music to her words. "Back home, we'd leave a candle in the window on Christmas Eve to guide Mary and Joseph." She placed a single candle on the windowsill.

Jewell, stringing cranberries for the tree, shared her own tradition. "In Louisiana, we'd have bonfires along the Mississippi to light the way for Papa Noel."

Kyra marveled at the rich tapestry of traditions, each thread weaving into the fabric of their shared celebration.

On the tufted sofa in the lobby, Declan's mother, Eleanor, sat surrounded by papers and lists, her brow furrowed in concentration.

"Kyra, dear," Eleanor called, waving her over. "We still need to decide on the flowers for your bouquet. And have you given any more thought to the music for the ceremony?"

Kyra's heart swelled with affection for her soon-to-be mother-in-law. Eleanor had welcomed her with open arms, accepting her past without judgment and embracing her as a daughter. It was a love that filled a void she hadn't realized existed.

"I was thinking maybe wildflowers," Kyra replied, settling beside Eleanor. "Something simple and natural, like Texas itself."

Eleanor beamed, patting Kyra's hand. "That sounds perfect, my dear."

The sound of boots on the wooden floor announced Declan's arrival. Kyra's heart skipped a beat as he entered, his presence still sending a thrill through her after all these months.

"Well, don't you ladies have this place looking like a proper

Christmas wonderland," he said, his eyes twinkling as they met Kyra's.

He moved to help Mei with a particularly stubborn garland, his tall frame easily reaching where she struggled. Kyra watched him, marveling at how naturally he fit into this world they were building together.

"How's the new house coming along?" Eleanor asked.

Declan grinned, pride evident in his voice. "The framing's up, and we should have the roof on before the New Year. That wrap-around porch is going to be something special, I tell you."

Kyra's heart fluttered at the thought of their future home. For now, she lived with Isabella and Eleanor in the house Declan had bought at the edge of town, while he stayed at his rooms in the hotel. It was a necessary propriety until they were wed, even if most of the town knew of Kyra's brief foray into the world of the Bluebonnet Belles.

"Any news on Isabella's divorce?" Kyra asked, her voice lowered.

Declan nodded, his expression turning serious.

"The solicitor thinks we've found a loophole. Your research has been invaluable, darling. We might be able to get her free without her having to move to Sioux Falls after all."

Pride swelled in Kyra's chest. Her ability to absorb legal knowledge and her knack for research had proven more useful than she'd ever imagined. After fighting for her own freedom, she was fighting for others, like Isabella.

The lobby doors swung open, and Scarlett and Clive walked in. They were deep in conversation about some business matter, but Clive's face lit up when he saw his family.

"Well, if it isn't my favorite soon to be sister-in-law," Clive teased, ruffling Kyra's hair affectionately. "Still putting up with this lug, are you?"

"Someone has to keep him in line," she retorted, winking at Declan.

Scarlett approached, a warm smile on her face. "Kyra, I wanted to tell you that the response to your school has been overwhelming."

Kyra beamed with pride. Her school for women had become more than she'd ever dreamed. Not only was she teaching women about the law and encouraging civic engagement, but she'd also started a discreet program to help women in unsavory marriages find a way out.

"I never imagined I'd be doing something like this," Kyra admitted. "But it feels right, like I've found my calling."

Declan appeared at her side, his hand resting lightly on the small of her back. "Kyra, could I borrow you for a moment? There's something I need to discuss with you in my office."

With a quick excuse to the others, Kyra followed Declan to the small office. As soon as the door closed behind them, he pulled her into his arms, his lips finding hers in a passionate kiss that left her breathless.

"I've been wanting to do that all day," he murmured against her lips.

Kyra's body molded to his as if they were made for each other. Their stolen moments were sweet torture, the anticipation of finally living under the same roof and not having to sneak around building with each passing day.

"I can't wait to wake up next to you every morning," she whispered, her fingers tracing the line of his jaw. "To fall asleep in your arms every night."

Declan's eyes darkened with desire. "Soon, my love. Very soon."

As they held each other, Kyra marveled at the journey that had brought her to this moment. She had come to Wylde seeking an escape from a loveless marriage, never imagining she would find not just freedom, but a love so deep it transformed her very soul.

"I never knew I was fighting for more than just myself," she said softly. "With the school, helping Isabella, being part of this family—I'm fighting for all the people I love now. And that list keeps growing, thanks to you."

Declan tenderly brushed a strand of hair from her face. "You've brought so much light into my life, Kyra. Into all our lives. I fall more in love with you every day."

Kyra's heart swelled. She had found more than just a husband in Declan—she'd found a partner, a best friend, and a champion for her dreams. He had brought her into a family that accepted and loved her unconditionally.

As they rejoined the others in the lobby, the air filled with laughter and the warm glow of candlelight, peace settled over her. This was home, she realized. Not just the building but the people within it. The family she had chosen, and who had chosen her in return.

The decorations sparkled, a visual representation of the joy that filled her heart. In three weeks, she would become Mrs. Declan Kent, but she was already part of something greater—a community, a family, a love that knew no bounds.

As Declan's arm slipped around her waist, she settled into him, and Kyra sent up a silent prayer of gratitude. For the journey that had brought her here, for the love that surrounded her, and for the future that stretched out before them, bright with promise and possibility.

Jack needed a man to work his farm. What he got was Jo—a spitfire from Manhattan. Will their fiery tempers burn them to ash or ignite their love?

Dive into **Breaking Josephine** the series starter of the *Forbidden Romances* series.

To find out about new releases, including the next book in the Bluebonnet Belles, *Scarlett and the Sheriff*, get exclusive content, and more sign-up for **Brooke Stanton's newsletter**!

If you have time to leave a review to help other readers fall in love with Kyra and Declan, you can do so at the retailer of your choice. It doesn't have to be long. Just a sentence or two. Readers like you will love ya for it.

ALSO BY BROOKE STANTON

The Forbidden Romance Series

(steamy historical westerns)

Breaking Josephine

He needed a man to work his farm. What he got was her—a spitfire from
Manhattan. Will their fiery tempers burn them to ash or ignite their
love?

Ruby's Passion

Moments after Ruby says I do, a secret rips her marriage apart. James is
haunted by his bride's discovery. Can their hearts be mended, or is all
hope lost?

Lucy's Awakening

She married him to save her family. He married her out of duty. What
happens when she breaks the rules and falls in love?

Saving Kimi

Two men want her heart. She wants freedom. Is it possible to accept
love, without losing it all?

Serena's Silence

A tragedy took her voice. He's heartbroken and damaged. Can his wounds be healed in time to break her silence?

Amy's Salvation

Her marriage is a sham. He's a brooding widower. Can they find love in an impossible situation?

Margaret's Rapture

She's young and jilted. He's a bitter country doctor. When they're forced together, their fiery hate turns to a fiery passion that they're helpless to resist.

Steamy Historical Western Romance Boxset

Grab books 1-4 in the Forbidden Romance Series (includes fun historical facts for each book)

<u>The Bluebonnet Series</u>

(steamy historical westerns)

Kyra and the Saloon Boss

He needed a man to work his farm. What he got was her—a spitfire from Manhattan. Will their fiery tempers burn them to ash or ignite their love?

Scarlett and the Sheriff

Coming Soon

<u>**Christmas Quickies**</u>

(steamy holiday novellas)

The Christmas Dare

Getting dumped at Christmas wasn't in Holly Winter's holiday plans—neither was sharing a cabin with her off-limits best friend, Finn Parker.

The Naughty List

She's a small-town firecracker. He's a big-city developer. This Christmas, their fiery clash will spark more than just a holiday war.

A Very Merry Meet-Cute

(Coming Soon)

<u>**The Bloom Sisters Series**</u>

(sweeter rom coms)

The Misadventures of Catie Bloom

Catie made a career out of lies. Sam's a sportswriter with a reputation. Can they fake it till they make it into each other's arms?

The Adventures of Natalie Bloom

Natalie's secretly in love with him. Max's ex wants him back. Will he see what's right in front of him before it's too late?

The Downfall of Catie Bloom

Her white lies have finally caught up to her. His ex is back. Can she salvage the pieces of her perfect life or has she lost it all?

Bloom Sisters Boxset

Grab all three books plus a bonus novella in one place for way less.

<u>The Madly Bad at Love Series</u>

(steamy rom-coms)

Unbossly Manners

Peyton's a bedroom novice. Jackson's stuck on his ex. But when Jackson becomes Peyton's sexual instructor, will sparks start to fly?

The Revenge Pact

When Eva discovers her man is cheating, it's time for war. Her mission: revenge. Her secret weapon: the lying bastard's grumpy best friend, Ethan.

Boss with Benefits

(coming soon)

Rachel's young and feisty. Derrick's a grumpy ex-detective and her boss. Can her fire melt his ice?

ACKNOWLEDGMENTS

They say it takes a village to raise a child, but let me tell you—it takes a whole dang wagon train to birth a book, especially if it's the start of a new series!

First and foremost, I need to tip my hat to my brilliant editors: Debi Dove, Chloe Hackland, and Bekky Cunningham. Thank you for catching all those anachronistic "anyways" and reminding me that, no, the hero wouldn't ride a stallion—because even though Declan is a *hot* stallion, the real horse would be too wild to tame.

To Mick, my amazing husband who has only ever read one of my books (and I like it that way): darling, thank you for never saying a word when it looks like a bomb has gone off in my life during those final deadline pushes. You're my real-life romantic hero, even if you refuse to wear the chaps I bought for "research purposes."

To my amazing (and sometimes crazy) children: thank you for understanding that Mommy's books are not for your eyes... yet. And God help me when one of your friends discovers the types of books I write.

To my Tuesday night writing group: For our dinners, our writing trip last year where we stayed across from a junkyard (*but if you look out the back window, it's like we're in an episode of Dawson's Creek, right?*), and for being part of my smut crew (I know, I know, not all of you write *smut*... but you should. ;)

And to anyone who's ever sat behind me at a coffee shop and never questioned when I googled "*slang for intercourse in the US in 1985.*"

And finally, to you, reader: Thank you. This book wouldn't exist without you. Just reading this book supports artists and helps bring my vision of steamy historical romance to the Wild West.

Thank you everyone for helping me wrangle this story into something that would make even the most hardened cowboy blush. Yeehaw!

ABOUT THE AUTHOR

Who knew a girl who used to stand on stage and sing opera would be sitting behind a desk "singing" other people's stories? Not me! But here I am.

I'm a mom of two young girls. Most days I look around and wonder how the hell I got into my own little groundhog day—get the kids ready, write, workout, clean the dishes, fold the laundry, taxi the kids to their activities, make dinner, read, sleep, rinse, repeat. My husband (who's Australian) says it's like the Harbor Bridge, every year the workers start repainting the bridge at one end and by the time they get to the other side, they have to start all over. Yeah. That's life with kids.

But how did I get here, an author telling other people's love stories? I moved to Manhattan straight out of college because my sister lived there and I could crash on her couch. I did a lot of 'research' in my twenties before moving to Los Angeles where I wrote a lifestyle column for an online newspaper. When I struggled with pregnancy, I turned to my two favorite things— writing and humor- and created *Vagina Vacancy*, a blog about the highs and lows of IVF.

Creative writing is my happy place, but it wasn't until I acquired an NYC lit agent that I realized writing could be a career. Unfortunately, the agent had to step away from publishing for personal reasons and I was left in a quandary. I had a manuscript I loved, but no one to sell it. That's when I joined my local RWA chapter and entered my manuscript into their contest. To my delight, the book received second place.

That was 2015 when indie publishing was on the rise, and my fellow authors told me—when done right—being your own boss could be lucrative. I was a quick writer and business-minded and starting my own publishing business felt like something I could excel at. So I took my award-winning manuscript, hired a team of editors, designers, and marketing gurus, and went to work. The first book was a bestseller and since then I've published two series and eight books—many of which have reached number one, woot!—and scooped up another award along the way.

When I'm not writing or parenting—the two things that take up most of my time—you can find me at the gym, meditating, going to a concert with my hubby, or drinking buckets of wine with my girlfriends.

If you wanna know more about me and my books check out my website brookestantonbooks.com or email me here hi@brooke stantonbooks.com.